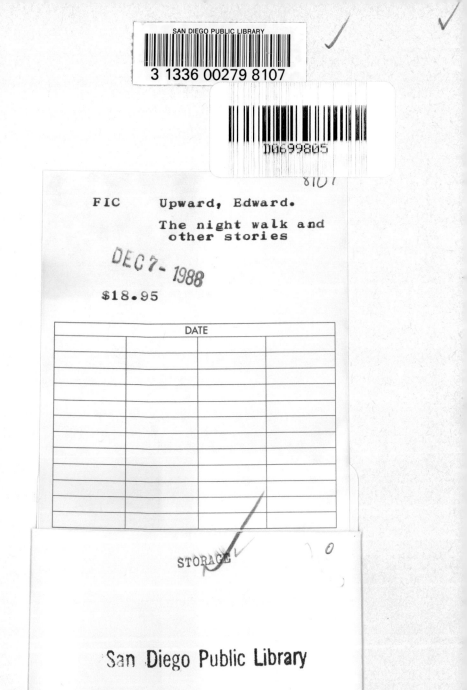

DATE		

*The Night Walk
and Other Stories*

Books by
EDWARD UPWARD

Journey to the Border
The Railway Accident and Other Stories
The Night Walk and Other Stories

The Spiral Ascent (trilogy)
In the Thirties
The Rotten Elements
No Home but the Struggle

EDWARD UPWARD

*The Night Walk
and Other Stories*

Heinemann : London

William Heinemann Ltd
10 Upper Grosvenor Street, London W1X 9PA
LONDON   MELBOURNE   AUCKLAND
JOHANNESBURG

This collection first published in Great Britain 1987
© Edward Upward 1979, 1980, 1981, 1984, 1985, 1987

SBN 434 81173 4

Photoset by Deltatype, Ellesmere Port,
Printed and bound in Great Britain by
Billing & Sons Limited, Worcester

CONTENTS

———

The author is grateful to the editors of the following magazines or journals in which some of the stories, or earlier versions of them, included in this collection, have previously appeared.

The London Magazine for 'Her Day' (November 1979); 'An Old-Established School' (April–May 1981); 'The Interview' (April–May 1984); 'At the Ferry Inn' (July 1985)

The Guardian for 'The Procession' (3 May 1980)

Nuclear Fragments, published by Earthright Publications, Newcastle, for 'Over the Cliff'

Adam International Review for 'The Spectacle' (1979)

Flashpoint for 'I Dreamt of a Valley' (September 1981)

The Leveller for 'Love is Nice'.

PN Review 19 for 'The Last Good Thing that a Bad Reporter Should Heed' (1980).

Also 'The White-Pinafored Black Cat' was read on BBC Radio 3 on 5 August 1985 in an abridged version under the title 'The Sister who Survived'.

To the memory of
Christopher Isherwood,
my friend for sixty-five years

Her Day

THE BEARERS carry the dead woman in her coffin out of the front door of her home and down the steps and through the gateway under the meeting branches of the laurustinus and the leafless lilac to the motor-hearse at the edge of the pavement. The husband and the two middle-aged sons follow soon afterwards when the gateway is clear, walking not slowly but ordinarily, as men whom ceremony embarrasses, and a little more quickly they get into the black Daimler limousine which is the only car behind the hearse. The proprietors of the private hotel across the road, Mrs Chedglow and Miss Frage, have come out into their front garden to show their respect and to watch the hearse with the coffin visible through its glass sides move off up the hill. For many months they have seen the woman go down on Sunday evenings to the post-box at the bottom of the hill, walking carefully because of her bandaged leg which ever since her cancer operation has become gradually more swollen, holding her letters up out of reach of the neighbourhood dogs, five or six of them, that have harassingly surrounded her most of the way down the hill and then up again and have barked without pause at the oddity of her lameness. Each day for several weeks Mrs Chedglow has cooked special meals which Miss Frage has taken across to her while she has lain on the long sofa in the drawing-room, unable any more to go upstairs or to stand at the stove in her kitchen. Now as the hearse followed by the one limousine is driven slowly away from the dead woman's home they do not try to keep out of their looks the disquiet which the smallness of the procession makes them feel.

There is no ambiguity of feeling in the faces of the two ageing road-sweepers who take off their caps and stand still, with their heads bowed and their hands resting on the tops of the handles of their brooms in front of them, when the hearse rounds the corner higher up the hill. The sympathy their tired features show is no mere conventional appearance assumed out of consideration for the relatives of the dead but reveals without reserve the sorrow of their own defeated lives. The face of the caretaker at the cemetery where the brothers went two days ago to make arrangements for their mother's grave had a similar look, and as they were leaving him he told them, 'Don't live to be old.' They did not suppose that he was advocating suicide or that he had ever thought of committing it himself. Nor would their mother have thought of it, in spite of all her griefs. She never wished to die – 'Death is not very nice', she once said when the two sons as young men were talking of the various modes of corpse disposal discussed by Sir Thomas Browne in his *Urne Buriall* – though she was not afraid of dying. Mrs Radnor, the home-help who recently had been coming to the house every morning, had reported to the younger son that his mother had said three days before her death, 'I think I may be going to shuffle off this mortal coil', strange words accurately remembered by Mrs Radnor who knew no Shakespeare. And the husband when opening his bureau the day after her death to look for notepaper and an envelope found her handbag there, and inside it a paperback detective novel – she didn't normally read such novels – and the title on the cover was *Appointment with Death*.

The hearse followed by the black limousine comes to a stop outside the lych gate of the Anglican parish church which the dead woman used to attend. The husband and the two sons feel surprise, since the arrangement is that there shall be no service in the church and that the burial shall take place at the municipal cemetery a quarter of a mile farther on. The road is narrower outside the church than elsewhere, because of the nearness of an old inn opposite, a building listed for preservation, and the traffic behind and in front of the hearse and the limousine has to slow down. Each car or commercial van which cautiously draws out to pass the two black stationary vehicles from behind, or decelerates when passing them from in front, could seem to downward-looking air-travellers like an individual ant pausing in a procession of ants to inspect momentarily the killed body of a member of its own colony. Then the hearse moves on again. The undertakers have not made a mistake, or if they have it has been a brief one. Perhaps the stop outside this church had a ritualistic purpose, was intended by them to signify that the dead woman used to worship there.

How much would she have minded if she could have known that her husband would decide against a full-length Anglican service? Did she ever believingly say to herself the words, 'I know that my Redeemer liveth, and though worms destroy this body, yet in my flesh shall I see God'? Words which whenever the elder son heard them sung by a woman in a performance of Handel's *Messiah* brought poignantly to him the thought of all the women whose only hope throughout the Christian ages had been of heaven, and whose wrongs and sufferings had been greater than men's. What she would have liked best, as she had made clear several times to her husband and to her sons – though she had never put it in her will, and even if she had he would have ignored it – was to have her ashes scattered on the downs. She was a romantic; and her romanticism was stronger than her Christianity, in which convention and class conformism had had at least as important a place as doctrine. But from her belief in the rightness of upper class attitudes she was never able, even when she was young, to break quite free. Her constant criticisms of the weaknesses of her husband and her sons may have been due to a need to compensate herself for her acceptance in principle of upper class and Christian insistence on the inferiority of woman to man.

Near the caretaker's lodge at the gates of the municipal cemetery the tall bare-headed vicar in his white surplice with his black cassock below it reaching down to his shoes is waiting for them. His face has a grey bleakness, appropriate to his function here this morning, but does it also show a resentment because of the shortening of the service? The bearers take up the coffin and he goes ahead of them up the gravel path of the cemetery. His voice rises startlingly in the open air of the chill blue December day: 'I am the resurrection and the life . . . and whosoever liveth and believeth in me shall never die'. Powerful words spoken now with power and with an appreciation of their sound as words by a man whom neither the husband nor the sons had hitherto suspected of loving the English language. A voice resonant and vehement above the graves, as though this man were thinking 'I'll show these cultured infidels what faith means.' And the elder son thinks, 'Which *sounds* better, these words or "Proletarians of all lands unite. . . . You have a world to win"?' He tells himself that the sound cannot be separated from the sense, and that human victory on earth is more possible than everlasting life elsewhere. The vicar turns and leads the way along one of the side paths among the gravestones, and the bearers follow. They come soon to an open grave, dug doubly deep so that there will be room for another coffin eventually, though the sons have not given instructions for this to be done and they can't imagine their father would have. The edges of the grave are fringed with bright green artificial grass to hide the trodden mud there, and its sides are very cleanly dug and have a slight shine on them like a polish transferred from the metal of the diggers' spades. The bearers let the coffin down into the grave on ropes, slowly, giving no sign of the muscular strain this must cause them. Now comes that part of the ceremony which the elder son has been expecting with most unease, the macabre casting of a handful of earth on to the lid of the coffin and the hollow noise that might reverberate out from the deep and narrow grave. But in the event the vicar's voice speaking the words 'dust to dust' makes the impact of the finely crumbled earth on the wood below seem hardly more audible than if the earth were in fact dust falling on dust.

When the ceremony is finished the husband followed by the sons approaches the vicar and walks slowly beside him without speaking for a while but at last says to him, 'She was eighty-two. We were married for fifty years.' The sons know that he has for the moment quite forgotten the quarrelling that went on between her and him so monotonously during so many of the days of those years. The vicar's look is only briefly less aloof than when he met them at the cemetery gates. They leave him soon and get into the black limousine once more, which takes them home less slowly than it brought them here. Just before it reaches their house they notice at the front window of the private hotel across the road the faces of Mrs Chedglow and Miss Frage showing shock and disapproval because this all too early return proves to them that there cannot have been a proper funeral service.

The father and the two sons step out of the black limousine and they walk more quickly back into the house than they came out of it. He takes off his overcoat, then goes upstairs, but the sons move along the hall passage towards the open door of the sunlit drawing-room, which their mother will not sit in again. They see on the white marble mantelshelf a photograph of her that they are sure was not there when they went into the room on the previous evening to look at her lying in the coffin. Even if Mrs Radnor could have found the photograph in a drawer, she would surely not have had the idea of putting it up there. They would not have supposed their father capable now of sentiment about their mother, but they realise that only he could have had this idea.

The photograph is circular in a rectangular green frame with small red flowerbud-like decorations at its corners. It shows her in her twenties, with a softly oval face and serious dark eyes and with copious dark hair held by a comb though astray here and there. The ends of a long black ribbon, satin or velvet, decending on either side of her rounded neck, meet and cross each other where a pierced circular silver ornament, asymmetrically placed just above the left side of her unemphasised bosom, holds them fastened to the loosely fitting Italian-seeming silk jacket she is wearing. The sons know that the asymmetry is unlikely to have been a fashion of the period when the photograph was taken, because if it had been she would almost certainly not have adopted it. She preferred to make her own fashions. She wanted to be different – and not only in the way she dressed – from the majority of the people she grew up among. When she was young she was able to do many of the things she wished to do. The sons feel no sadness but an intensifying gladness as they see her now in her beauty and in her freedom. This is how they will most often remember her after today.

The Procession

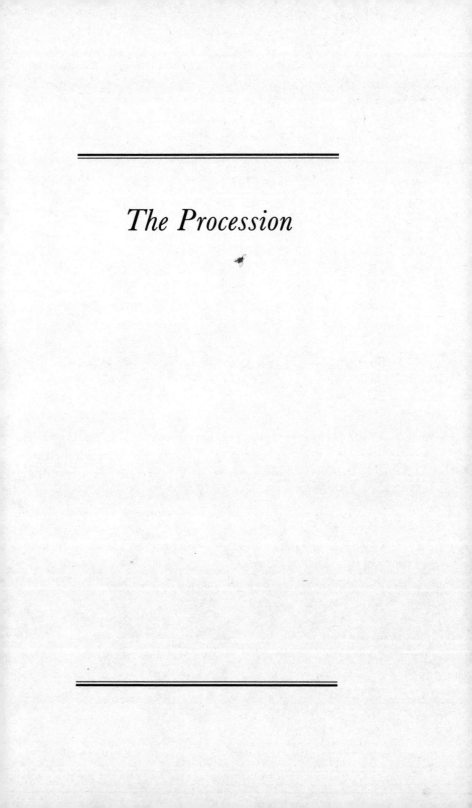

On a balustered balcony five storeys or more above the unexpectedly crowdless street I stood waiting for a procession which I foreknew would be significantly unlike the Lord Mayor's Show my mother had lifted me up to look at from a similar balcony in my early childhood seventy years before. What I was about to see now might be a military parade or a funeral or a political demonstration rather than a carnival of any kind. It seemed a long time coming. When I stopped staring up the street for a while I noticed that I was by myself on the balcony and that a stone ledge extending from one side of this along the face of the building as far as another balcony at the same height fifteen yards away might not be broad enough to give a hesitating suicide a foothold for more than a few seconds, and could be slippery too with all the grey-white excrement deposited there by night-roosting starlings. A gilded spike pointing up towards me from the top of the lantern of an iron street-lamp far below must have held my interest for longer than I was aware, because when I looked away along the street again the first walkers in the procession were already very near.

Walkers, not marchers. Without music from drums or fifes or brass. No one was singing or shouting. And there were no small bright balloons with faces or slogans colour-printed on them floating from strings above the faces of the walkers, no flowery tableaux formed by tiaraed young girls in rising tiers on lorries with decorated wheels like revolving rosettes, no huge wicker-work or papier-mâché images of Gog and Magog or of John Bull. But if I was seeing a funeral it was not a state ceremony in which a riderless horse with reversed Wellington boots fixed to the stirrups would be followed by a flag-draped coffin on a gun-carriage. Although the walkers were so noiseless along the street that I could almost have supposed the women as well as the men must be wearing rubber soles and heels, they were casually dressed and did not try to keep in step with one another, or they might even – as anti-militarists – be purposely keeping out of step. It could be a political demonstration. I thought I recognised a fair-haired girl there who when I met her once at a left-wing meeting had told me I was her favourite painter, and I had believed her. I was sure that the two exceptionally tall young men in the procession, not walking together nor seeming to be known to each other, were two students, a Latvian and a New Zealander, who had on separate occasions come to ask me questions about the relationship between politics and art, my art in particular, and I had called them 'giants' afterwards when I had described them to my friends. But if I was watching a demonstration why were there no banners? There was only an unframed painting on canvas which one of the walkers was holding up by its lowest corners. Its prevailing colour was woodland green, and it was frighteningly familiar, yet I could not wholly understand what made me afraid until I saw coming on close behind the painting, and pushed like a barrow by three or four of the walkers, a low-wheeled vehicle carrying an exposed coffin. Though the lid was not, as in a Greek Orthodox Church funeral, removed from the coffin, I knew whose corpse was inside.

The voice of my dear love who was standing suddenly

quite near me said consolingly to me, 'We never expected we would be lucky enough to go together. One of us had to be first. I wish it had been me, just as you would have wished it had been you if it had been me.' Before I could turn towards her I heard myself crying out in protest to all the street, 'I don't want to die yet. There's no reason why I should be dead now. I haven't been ill or in an accident.' When I did turn to her she was not there, must have gone back into the large room which led out through wide-open French windows on to the balcony. But my cry had been heard by the broad-bodied elderly man in a conspicuously well-tailored suit who was coming along the balcony from the room unhurriedly towards me. I was in no doubt that he was Everard Axtell, who had been my friend when we were younger. The brightly flower-patterned shirt he wore now might seem too young for his hair which had become entirely white, but his features had aged so little that he would have been instantly recognisable by me even if I hadn't seen recent photographs of him so often in the newspapers. He took a second or two to recognise me, then said, 'That funeral is not yours.'

There was a kindliness rather than any real kindness in his voice. He could have been a professional healer speaking to someone unwell. 'If the funeral were yours you would not be standing on the balcony here. You would be down there in the coffin.' As though he thought I was insufficiently impressed by his reasoning, he went on with less kindliness, 'You will never have a public funeral, not even a third-rate cockney one such as you have been watching.' I became aware of him as having the kind of face and figure which would have made him appear 'distinguished' even to people who had never heard of him. He could have been taken for a famous former rugby player – a three-quarter back more probably than a forward, since he was not tall – or a diplomat, instead of the well-known art critic and collector he actually was. But it came to me that what he had been saying could be true, and evidently he guessed he was beginning to convince me; his voice changed, was more kindly again. 'You might have been able to expect to have a public funeral some day, though only a small and unofficial one, if you'd gone on painting in the style you'd already begun to develop in your early twenties.' I still said nothing. He asked with genuine but controlled exasperation, 'Why did you abandon the kind of realistic fantasy you were capable of when you painted *The Wormhouse Gate*?'

I wondered whether what exasperated him might mainly be that he thought of me as having thrown away a capability he wished he himself had possessed.

'I doubt whether I know why,' I said.

'We all of us admired that picture. Admittedly we saw an element of parody in it which bordered on farce here and there. The violent viridian of the moss on the huge rocks among the oak trees obviously referred to some of Courbet's forest scenes – I remember how highly you thought of him as a painter then – but whereas his forests give an impression which is anything but peaceful and one feels that a sportsman's gun might be fired from behind a tree at any moment, your oak spinney is almost ludicrously' – Axtell spoke that word in a complimentary tone – 'sinister, as if somewhere in it just out of sight a poacher was about to step unawares into an iron-toothed mantrap; and I find it quite miraculous that at the same time we are somehow reminded – perhaps it's a case of extremes inevitably suggesting their opposites – of the dreamily hazy springtime leaves in a Corot birch wood. Was there a sapling in the left foreground of your picture with a few very small rhomboidally-shaped leaves growing on it?'

'Yes there was.'

14

'Well, that may partly account for the Corot effect. But of course the central thing in the whole design is the Poussin-like sepulchre glimpsed between oak-trunks in the middle-distance. One can imagine one sees the words *Et in Arcadia Ego* incised in the stone lintel over the sepulchral doorway, yet when one looks closely the lettering turns out to be nothing more than accidental vertical markings on the stone, and the lintel itself is only a horizontal slab of rock which some geological happening has left balanced over a door-like boulder. And the Arcadian shepherds one thought were there on either side of the doorway are just not there at all; nor is the medieval Mayday morning party of horse-riders whose bright clothes – malachite green for the women and gold on blue for the men – seemed distantly visible in the sunlit interstices between tree trunks at the farthest edge of the spinney; nor is the early twentieth century one-cylinder motor-car which had appeared to be coming along the palely buff-coloured lane you placed near the righthand lower corner of the picture, though some rather shapeless dark vehicle is in fact represented at that point. And there are other objects and people and also animals – from various historical and pre-historical epochs – you managed to suggest and bring together in this painting without actually representing them. You were called a surrealist by some critics at the time, but I think this was a complete misnomer. You were essentially a representationalist, and nothing physically impossible or even improbable was depicted in any of your paintings – such as women with knob-handled chests-of-drawers in place of bosoms, or giraffes with their manes on fire. But you were a representationalist of a new kind. You were unique.'

I couldn't help showing the gratification he made me feel, but my feeling was quickly changed by what he said next:

'Why didn't you develop that style farther instead of going

on to produce the flat and unallusive naturalistic stuff you've confined yourself to for the last twenty-five years – utterly without undertones or overtones or warmth or atmosphere or wit, bare of all feelings except the most commonplace and dubious political ones?'

'I couldn't have gone on in my earlier style however much I'd wanted to. I couldn't have ignored how shallow and false it was as a response to the real horrors of the contemporary external world. Some art critics may think that art needn't tell the truth about any reality outside itself, but I think that if it doesn't it becomes fraudulent not just morally but also as art.' Not caring whether he might assume that the anger I knew I was failing to disguise might be due simply to his having wounded my personal vanity, I continued: 'I wanted my paintings to deal with things of fundamental concern to ordinary people today and I wanted to paint in a way which would be generally intelligible. I didn't want to be the kind of painter who disguises his lack of content by being superficially as elaborate as possible.'

Axtell appeared not to have been listening to me. 'If you'd gone on in your earlier style,' he said, 'you could have been at least a partial success, like – ' he paused and then named two names which, though he spoke them clearly enough and though I felt they ought to be familiar to me, I couldn't recognise. But I was certain that neither of the names was his own. He hadn't paused out of modesty. I could see that he thought of himself not as a partial but as a complete success. At the same moment I noticed a decoration pinned to the cloth of his suit just above the breast pocket – a ribbon with a garish and cheap-looking medal attached to it. Presumably it had been awarded to him by the State and presented by the Monarch. I thought, 'You did not cost them much', and I had a quick temptation to speak these words aloud, but I was helped to restrain myself by remembering how unseemly and sordid it is when old friends quarrel with one another in old age, and the words were driven utterly out of my mind by my sudden realisation that the painting of mine he had just been describing – *The Wormhouse Gate* – was the same one that had been carried by a walker in the funeral procession.

I jumped forward towards the balustrade, ignoring Axtell, and I leant over the white stone coping to stare after the procession which by now had moved on so far down the street that I couldn't be sure whether I saw where the coffin was any longer. I cried out in agony, 'It *is* my corpse they are carrying there.'

'No, it is not yours.' The voice that said this from behind me wasn't Axtell's. I turned and saw a very old man, short and thin and strikingly insignificant-looking compared with Axtell (who was no longer on the balcony), and I knew him at once as J. R. Sedgely, whom I revered more than any other painter of the twentieth century.

'It is not yours,' he said again. 'It is the corpse of the better artist you had it in you to be, but never were.' I was conscious of the characteristic slight lopsidedness of the features of his understanding face as he went on, 'Don't think I'm one of those who praise the richness of your younger style in order to seem all the more unprejudiced when they completely damn your maturer plainness. I don't doubt at all that your later paintings are better than your earlier, though those had something of imaginative value which if you had been able to retain and develop and meld it into your later work could have put you not in the first but in the second rank at least of the European painters of the last two centuries.'

I looked at him with gratitude, believing he meant what he said though I did not believe it to be true; but I said nothing.

'It is the same for all of us – not just the artists, but everyone alive in this century, even the luckiest of the lucky, and three quarters of the human population of the earth are not among the lucky. We are none of us able to be what we have it in us to be. It is the same for me.'

'No, no,' I passionately said. 'You are one of the truly great.'

'I don't think so. I have no illusions about my work.'

Mildly smiling he moved away from me and went in through the opened French windows at the back of the balcony. I followed him quickly, but not quickly enough. A wide and jagged crack appeared on the stone floor in front of the windows, and it rapidly deepened and lengthened along the whole balcony, which began to tilt downwards. I knew that within seconds I must fall into the street and be killed.

This was not a dream. I have invented it, with help from an actual nightmare I had in bed at home several years ago. It is a fantasy, and not even a realistic one. Yet it may convince me I can after all tell the truth about reality in a style that comes more readily to me than naturalism.

An Old-Established School

Quite soon on the first morning of term at an old-established school a temporarily appointed elderly schoolmaster, Henry Mitchell, realised that a number of the pupils were referring to him among themselves as Austerlyn Greenholt. The name was spoken in matter-of-fact tones, not disrespectfully at all, by someone in each of several groups of adolescent boys and girls who were lounging against multiple-shafted Victorian gothic pillars as he walked along the cloisters to look for the classroom where he was due to begin his teaching at this school. He did not resent the name – it was like an amalgam of two or three eminent names he couldn't immediately remember, and he was even a little pleased he was going to be known by it here (after all, he had been called worse things at some other schools) – nevertheless the promptness with which it had been invented could indicate a spiritedness among the pupils that he might do well to be wary of in good time. Unfortunately he would be less punctual in finding those of them who were waiting for him unsupervised in the classroom now than he need have been if the Headmaster's directions to him about how to get there had been less perfunctory.

He passed a pillar behind which a boy and girl were embracing each other, or rather the girl was embracing the boy, who stood still with a smirk on his face. Austerlyn's pretending not to notice them was made easier by the approach towards him at the same moment of another boy, tall and serious-faced, who said to him politely, 'The form you will be taking are in there, sir,' pointing to an arched doorway twenty yards in front of them along the cloisters. This boy – he was presumably the form-captain – walked slightly ahead of Austerlyn until they reached the doorway, where he stood aside to let the master go in first. It was not a classroom that Austerlyn came into but the Great Hall of the school. It seemed larger than any school assembly hall he had been in before, with what looked like a church organ at the farther end of it and at the nearer end a high gallery from the middle of the bow-shaped front of which a white clock-face mercilessly stared, and overhead there was a shadowy hammer-beamed roof. The form that had been waiting for him appeared to him at first sight to be a fairly small one – the appearance being no doubt due both to the comparatively little space its members took up in the Hall and to their orderliness as they sat there – but he soon estimated without having to count them that they might be as many as thirty-five, the boys and girls sitting in separate groups mainly, though there were a few pairs. He beckoned to the form-captain, who was on his way to sit down with the rest of the form.

'I understand this is to be a Chemistry lesson,' Austerlyn said, and the absurdity of it struck him even more now he was in this Hall than it had done when the Head had told him it was to be so. Austerlyn had raised the objection that he was not qualified to teach Chemistry but the Head had insisted, saying that this was only a 'one-off occasion' (what an expression for the Head of such a school as this to use, – or was the school, which had recently become co-educational, not really of the old-fashioned kind that Austerlyn had expected?) and the Head had finally added, giving Austerlyn a positively admiring smile, 'with your long experience you should have no difficulty in improvising.'

The tall form-captain looked respectfully puzzled, and said, 'Mr Birkett, our form-master, told us we were to bring our Geography exercise books and atlases, sir.'

'Well,' Austerlyn said, raising his voice so that other members of the form would be able to hear, 'the Headmaster told *me* it was to be Chemistry. And that's what it will be.'

He was suddenly glad of this. He had already improvised quite a bit of the lesson in his mind while he had been finding his way to the form he was now with. He would talk about the lives of famous chemists, or at least about those aspects of their lives which most interested him and which he knew a little about. Starting with Robert Boyle, mentioning the famous law about the relation of the volume and pressure of gases (but no more than mentioning it, since he had long ago forgotten its details) then concentrating on Boyle's battle against the obstinately surviving reactionary alchemical concepts of his day, such as the four elements. This would enable Austerlyn to generalise for a while on the entrenched prejudices which new ideas had come up against in every age. Next, Joseph Priestley, who discovered oxygen and had his house set on fire by the Church and Crown mob because of his sympathy with the French Revolution. What a pity Austerlyn would not be able to mention Gay-Lussac, about whom he knew nothing except his fascinating name.

He moved away from the form-captain and advanced towards the form. He came to a stop facing the middle of their front row. He raised his head and took into his view the whole thirty-five of them, individuals with interesting and even startling differences between them, but he felt he must be seen to see them as a group or else he might fail to get their full attention as individuals. He found he had stopped directly in front of an adolescent girl the skin of whose face had an astonishing baby-like delicacy of colour and texture. Just in case he might give the impression of having placed himself there not by accident but because she was attractive to him (as she was), he shifted his position quickly – though avoiding precipitancy – nearer to the rather heavy-faced boy who sat next to her. He spoke to the form as a whole, clearly and no more loudly than was necessary to reach their back row.

'I am going to talk to you this morning about the lives of famous chemists. There was a time not long ago when such a topic might have been considered out of place in a Chemistry lesson. It certainly would have been considered out of place as long ago as when I attended my first Chemistry lesson.' He noticed no smiles anywhere along the four rows in which the form sat. 'Strangely enough I was quite excited at the idea of learning science – before I actually started learning it.' There was not a single snigger or titter from any of them. And very rightly. He knew that by suggesting there had been something odd about his having been keen to learn science at school he was trying to ingratiate himself with them in a quite disgraceful way; and, worse still, if the cap of his criticism happened to fit the chemistry-teaching at this school and his new colleagues got to hear of what he'd said, he might be held guilty of unprofessional conduct. But he couldn't prevent himself from adding, 'Chemistry soon came to seem nothing more to me than Bunsen burners and pipettes and litmus paper and substances in bottles which had nothing to do with life outside the lab.' The form looked monolithically stolid. He turned away from them and took a pace or two in the direction of that end of the Hall where the gallery was, with its merciless white-faced clock. Movement, he knew from experience, was often a useful ploy (what a word, but he had found lately that slang could sometimes help his thinking) to hold attention at moments when he wasn't sure what he wanted to say next. He saw, below and in front of the gallery, a large blackboard and easel. Almost surprised that someone had had the forethought to provide this, he went forward to it. He was oddly confident that no one in the form was playing up behind his back. There was even a new stick of yellow chalk ready for him – it had been placed on the thick felt of a new board-duster, which was tri-coloured like a dingy neapolitan ice, and the wooden holder of the duster had been carefully balanced on one of the pegs that held up the board. The names of two more chemists came quickly into his mind. Lavoisier and Cavendish. He would tell the form that it was Lavoisier who totally and finally overthrew the phlogiston theory which Boyle's experiments had already called in question, and they would be interested to hear that Cavendish discovered hydrogen which led to early experiments with balloons, and he could tell them a thing or two about Cavendish's eccentric private life as well. He turned to face the form again, and their unshifting gaze convinced him that their eyes must have been on him all the time he had been walking away from them towards the blackboard.

He wrote the name Robert Boyle in large script at the top of the board. He began to speak about Boyle, more loudly than he had spoken about his own first experience of Chemistry lessons, but not more loudly than he saw was sufficient now to be clearly heard by the listeners in the back row. Yet before long he found he had to raise his voice a little, and then again a little. He didn't immediately know why he felt that this increase of volume was necessary. The form were not beginning to show any obvious signs that he was becoming inaudible to them. At last he noticed there was another sound competing with the sound of his voice; and its volume must be increasing at a faster rate than he was achieving, otherwise he might have noticed it even less soon. The noise did not come from the form, was not any kind of visually undetectable subversive humming. It did not come from anywhere inside the Hall, but from the cloisters outside. It was produced by the footsteps and voices of another form who now arrived at the open doorway and entered the Hall, becoming quiet as they did so. At their rear was a woman teacher; and while they walked on quietly to seat themselves near the other end of the Hall, well beyond the form that Austerlyn was in charge of, she detached herself from them and came towards him. She was dark-haired, about thirty years old and so startlingly beautiful that he averted his eyes, though only for a moment, from her face just before she spoke to him:

'I'm so sorry about this, but I'm afraid it's quite typical of the way things go on the first morning of term here. Particularly at the beginning of a new school-year.'

'Oh that's quite all right,' he said, not averting his eyes.

She was obviously well aware of her beauty, but altogether indifferent to it at present or to its effect on him. She saw him as a colleague, which he knew was how he ought to see her.

'Operation Chaos we call this,' she said.

'Well, I'll admit I was slightly surprised to be asked to give a lesson in Chemistry, which I'm ignorant of, and to discover I had to give it in this Hall.'

'I hope my voice from the other end of the Hall won't distract you.' She certainly didn't mean to use that word in the way it could have been taken by him.

'And I hope my lesson won't disturb yours.'

'No problem,' she said.

With a colleaguely smile she went away from him towards her group of pupils – she seemed to have even more than he had – who had sat down in rows with their backs to his lot and at a distance of some ten yards from them. He began to speak again about Boyle, but before long he became conscious of someone moving – or hesitating – just outside the open doorway. How many more interruptions would there be? His concentration on what he was saying about Boyle was not helped by the fact that the hesitater now stopped moving altogether and simply stood there in the doorway. Austerlyn abruptly decided it would be better to change this lesson from Chemistry to Geography, for which the form had atlases they could study while he was coping with the next interruption. He walked up to them to tell them what he had decided and why. They showed no surprise. He could not discover from any of their faces whether what he had been saying about Boyle had interested them much, but he sensed that the impression he had made on them, so far, had not been a bad one. He asked them to find the map of South East Asia in their atlases. He already knew he had something which interested him so much more deeply than Chemistry to say about this part of the world that he couldn't fail to arouse an answering interest in it among them.

He would still need the blackboard. He liked to draw large rough sketch maps; and the speed of his drawing would excuse the inaccuracies his watchers ought to detect in the map he intended to draw now. As he walked away from the form again he saw that whoever had been standing in the doorway was no longer there. He went up to the blackboard and taking hold of the neapolitan felt duster he wiped off the name of Robert Boyle. Without speaking he rapidly sketched a map showing the boundaries of Vietnam, Laos and Kampuchea, and he wrote the names of these countries within their boundaries. He began to talk of the terrible destruction that had been done there by the richest and most powerful nation in the world. He noticed that someone was standing in the doorway again. It was a boy, rather shorter than most of the boys belonging to the form he was speaking to but probably not younger than they were, though his cheeks were remarkably rounded and rubicund. Austerlyn all at once recognised him as the boy he had seen being embraced by a girl behind a pillar in the cloisters.

Although the girl's face hadn't been turned away from Austerlyn, not much of it had been visible to him except a softly swelling palely pink cheek and the corner of a large dark eye and of opened lips more deeply red even than the boy's face, which she was avidly kissing the unviewable farther side of, while her hands reached under the boy's open jacket and were stroking the sides of his brown woollen pullover with a slow circular movement. His smirk had had conceit in it, but also just a little embarrassment, as if he hadn't been totally sure he wasn't being made a monkey of. His face still showed a smirk as he stood in the doorway now, yet this time he was quite unembarrassed. Austerlyn stopped speaking to the form and directed an expectant glance at the boy, who made no response to it although he certainly saw it; but after a delay which was long enough to make the point that he was in no way influenced by Austerlyn's glance he strolled into the Hall.

He came directly towards Austerlyn at first, then went behind him, passing however in front of the blackboard which Austerlyn had stepped away from at the moment of ceasing to speak to the form. The boy's head, with its cheeks showing more shinily red than ever against the board, performed a sudden jerky stiff-necked quarter-turn, like the manipulated head of a ventriloquist's dummy, and faced the form with a fixed grin of such pertness that Austerlyn could hardly keep his anger cold as he said to the boy:

'You're rather late for this lesson, aren't you?'

Instead of saying anything to Austerlyn, and without even looking at him, the boy gave the form a crude and slow wink from one of his abnormally long-lashed eyes. This time

Austerlyn spoke to him with a hard sharpness.

'What is your name?'

It seemed that the boy was going to ignore the question, but that suddenly he had a better idea.

'Laos,' he said.

'Repeat that,' Austerlyn said, controlling fury in case he might have misheard or in case Laos might by an almost incredible coincidence be the actual name of the boy and not an invention suggested to him by Austerlyn's having spoken it, and written it on the board, as the name of a country in South East Asia.

The boy walked on without answering and went to sit down at the right-hand end of the front row of the form Austerlyn was in charge of – the end which was farthest from the door and had no doubt been purposely chosen by the boy so that the progress of his late arrival in the Hall could be fully observed by the maximum number of his fellow pupils.

'I asked you to repeat your name,' Austerlyn said, in a tone he tried to make quieter than before, not wanting to heighten the drama of a scene he now sensed that the boy might have planned in advance.

The boy surprised him by answering this time at once that his name was Laos. However he pronounced it almost as one syllable – not Lah-oss now but Louss. Or Louse. He swivelled his wide-eyed gaze through ninety degrees along the front row of the form as if appealing for confirmation from them that he was telling the truth.

'It seems a remarkably appropriate name,' Austerlyn was horrified to hear himself say. Even if the name was a fake – which Austerlyn was nearly as certain it must be as he was of the impossibility of miracles – he had reacted to it in the worst way he could have: he had fallen into the double trap of allowing himself to be provoked by it and of being guilty himself of the cheapest and nastiest kind of traditional schoolmasterly provocation in return. And suppose that – by one chance in a billion – the name was not a fake: he would be guilty not merely of schoolmasterly sarcasm but of something that could almost be called inhumanity.

The boy did not respond for several seconds. Then he got quickly up from his seat and said loudly, though without shouting:

'Say that again, you wet geriatric slug, and I'll bash your face in.'

He came forward towards Austerlyn, who stood completely moveless trying to feel an absolute confidence that even at the present stage of world history his position as schoolmaster, if not his elderliness, still had sufficient charisma to inhibit any pupil from attempting an actual physical assault on him. The office makes the man and a dog's obeyed in office, he might have thought if he had had time to think, though he might also have remembered how in revolutionary periods be-medalled generals who have expected that their mere arrival upon the scene of a mutiny would be enough to quell it have been hauled from their horses and trampled to death by their men. But the boy, instead of trying to hit Austerlyn's face, walked straight past him, rather fast, and towards the doorway of the Hall.

Within a second or two Austerlyn, in rising rage, moved very rapidly after him, shouting from behind him, 'You will come with me at once to the Headmaster.'

The boy walked on and out into the cloisters, ignoring the shout. Austerlyn stopped in the doorway, realising that to go to the Headmaster's study would mean abandoning the form here in the Hall; and what would the Head think if he were to admit – as he could hardly avoid admitting – that he had been almost obscenely sarcastic about the boy's name, even if it was an impudently invented name?

Austerlyn turned and was beginning to walk slowly

towards the form, trying to re-assume an outward calmness, when he noticed that he was still holding the board-duster and the stick of chalk, the duster in his left hand and the chalk in his right. He would have liked to take these back to the board at once, but he was deterred by the thought that he might not succeed in getting the duster to balance on the peg where he had found it and that the form would see him ridiculously juggling with it for a second or two in a useless attempt to catch it as it dropped to the floor. He went forward and put it and the chalk down quickly on an unoccupied chair not far from the door. The form were all of them watching him. He looked at them and was unable to discover from their faces anything of what they felt about him and Laoss. He saw no blatant signs of gloating. They could not be expected to take the side of a master – and a stranger too – against one of themselves, yet Laoss might be a type who would not be particularly popular among them. They might not be against Austerlyn, even though they couldn't be for him. He got the impression that if he had been capable now of going on with this lesson about South East Asia they would have been willing enough to listen to him. But instead he told them, as unshakily as he could:

'I want each of you to make a map of the three countries I have sketched on the blackboard. Consult your atlases, and you can use tracing paper, if you have some with you, to draw the outlines. Put in the main towns and the main physical features – rivers and mountains.'

It might be rather too elementary a task for a form of adolescents, he suspected, but fortunately they didn't appear to think so. They all had tracing paper with them and they got down to work promptly, though they had nothing to rest their atlases on except their knees. He walked slowly along their front row and back again, as if he was an invigilator at an examination, and his movement lulled the hurt that sulked in his nerves. Then the thought came to him that the woman teacher, whose presence in the Hall he had completely forgotten during the past few minutes, was likely to have been aware of at least something of what had happened between him and Laoss. He looked up over the heads of the form towards the far end of the Hall; and she was on the platform there, facing the large group she was in charge of, but not talking to them at the moment. Her control over them was evidently such that she would have had leisure to watch anything going on at his end of the Hall, if she had wanted to, though now she was watching them not him. The silent organ with its many pewter-coloured pipes of varying widths and heights looming behind her at the back of the platform made her seem like a singer on the stage of a concert hall, a famous soprano about to begin to sing an aria, while the awed music from the orchestra had become so pianissimo that he could not hear it at all. But the appearance she had of being totally unconscious of him at his end of the Hall convinced him she must have seen and heard every shameful detail of the Laoss incident.

He turned his back on her and on the form. He was incapable even of pretending to continue to take an interest in their map-drawing. The large white-faced clock, unavoidably visible in the middle of the bow-shaped front of the gallery above and beyond the blackboard towards which he paced now, startled him momentarily by showing that thirty-five of the forty-five minutes allotted for this lesson had already passed; but there were still ten more to go. Bitterness made him indifferent to what the form might do in that remaining time. He cared only about what he would do when the ten minutes ended: he would see the Headmaster, give instant notice, get away from the school for ever this afternoon, regardless of breach of contract and loss of salary. What was he doing here anyway? Why was he continuing to teach at his age? Why was he allowed to? He should have stopped years ago. He didn't need the money. Yet he went on and on, and at every school where he got a job he had to endure some vile humiliation sooner or later. It had happened here on the first morning and it could soon happen again if he didn't escape without delay. It might be happening at this moment.

There was a noise behind him and he turned and saw that the form were beginning to stand up from their seats. They did not look as though they were conscious of acting rebelliously, nevertheless it was obvious they were about to make their way out of the Hall. They moved unhurriedly towards the doorway. One of them even came back from there, threading his way through the others who were going out; he might have left his atlas behind and be returning to fetch it. Perhaps ten minutes had passed more quickly than Austerlyn had realised, and the form were leaving the Hall quite legitimately to go to their next lesson. Or at least they would be leaving legitimately if he had given them the signal to dismiss. Perhaps he had given it, unintentionally, by some accidental movement he might have made with his arm in the agitation of his feelings after he had turned his back on them and on the woman teacher. It was too late to stop them now: most of them were already out in the cloisters – although one of them hadn't yet begun to move from the Hall, was standing near the front row of seats at the end farthest from the doorway. This was a boy, possibly the one who had returned while the rest of the form were walking out. He seemed to be waiting for Austerlyn. He was Laoss.

His stance wasn't aggressive. He was not staring directly at Austerlyn but at the floor between them. It was possible he had decided that he couldn't escape the consequences of his offence against Austerlyn and that he might as well surrender to him now. His face offered no show of contriteness, but the pertness and insolence had quite gone from it. Austerlyn suddenly suspected, without knowing why, that the name Laoss was more likely than not to be the boy's real name after all. And perhaps the others called him Louse and this had caused him to have a chip on his shoulder and to behave in the objectionable way he did. Austerlyn moved a few short steps towards him, stopped while there were still several yards between them, then spoke:

'I am very sorry for what I said to you. I am very sorry. I ought never to have said it.'

The boy gave no kind of response.

'I suppose I thought you were much younger than you are.' This sounded as though Austerlyn was trying to justify himself, and also it could be taken as an insult, and anyway no matter how young the boy's face might look or how short his body might be – though his shoulders were broad – there could be no excuse for the disgusting sarcasm Austerlyn had said he was sorry for. He continued quickly:

'I'm not asking you to forgive me. That would be just as impertinent as if I were to say I forgive you.'

The boy came towards Austerlyn, in an unaggressive way, but said nothing, and still without looking at him walked past him in the direction of the doorway. At least he would know now that he wasn't going to be punished, Austerlyn thought with a little relief, watching him go out into the cloisters and noticing at the same time that the form which the woman teacher had been in charge of were also on their way out through the doorway. Then he noticed she was standing beside him.

She said with colleaguely sympathy:

'He's a problem all right, that lad. I know him well. He was in my form all last year. But I must say he surprised even me this morning.'

Austerlyn would have liked to ask her whether the boy's

name really was Laoss, but if he did she might get on to talking about the boy in detail, and this would be repugnant to Austerlyn at present.

'I was as much to blame as the boy was,' he said.

'I think it was just one of those things that can always happen in our profession,' she said consolingly, though not contradicting him. 'They must have been happening for centuries, long before this school was rebuilt in Queen Victoria's reign and even before 1588 when it is said to have been founded.' She smiled. 'But formerly the taught and not the teachers were the ones who got hurt most.'

He had a brief impression that the Great Hall, now when her pupils as well as his had all made their way out of it, had become larger than ever, and its hammer-beams higher and shadowier.

'I was never cut out to be a teacher,' he said.

'You may say so, but I couldn't help listening to your lesson when I ought to have been minding my own business with my own class, and I watched your lot while you began to speak to them about South East Asia, as well as earlier on before you stopped speaking to them about Robert Boyle, and perhaps you didn't get through to all of them, but to some of them you did, and certainly to me.'

He said in a more relaxed tone than he had been capable of before:

'The trouble about taking temporary jobs in schools is that the pupils are apt to regard an elderly newcomer rather as they would a student-teacher, and he has to prove to them as soon as possible that he isn't fair game.'

'I'm sure that's not how they regard you here in this school.' She smiled again. 'If they did they might not have found such a distinguished-sounding name for you as the one I've overheard some of them using.'

She evidently kept her ears as well as her eyes open, he

thought, though he wasn't in the least riled by her referring so uninhibitedly to the fact that the pupils had given him a name which wasn't his own. And she went on:

'Have you been called Austerlyn Greenholt at any other school before this?'

'No. Why?'

'Well, such things can travel. In no time and from one end of the country to the other.'

Abruptly yet vaguely he remembered a school where just before leaving he had heard the name Austerlyn Greenholt spoken but had not connected it with himself. Instead of telling her this he said with some vigour:

'As soon as my three weeks at this school are up I shall retire from teaching for good.' Then he realised that his talking with her had at least saved him from carrying out his irresponsible intention of giving notice to the Head at once and leaving the school this afternoon.

'I don't imagine you will really retire, even when you're no longer a schoolmaster,' she said. 'You may believe you're not cut out for teaching, yet my guess is you will want to go on with it – not for teaching's sake but because of something you feel you need to teach, though I expect you will teach it mostly to adults and not in any educational institution.'

He looked at her and was aware again, as he had failed to be while his disgraceful confrontation with the boy still dominated his feelings, of the extraordinary beauty of her face.

'You are too sensitive, Henry,' she said.

She moved nearer to him, and leaning forward she kissed him warmly on the cheek. Too soon she stepped back from him and said, 'Now I must get along to my next class.' She walked away briskly towards the doorway of the Hall, allowing him no time even to ask how she had got to know his real forename. But as she went out of the doorway she gave him a quick colleaguely smile before she disappeared along the cloisters. He was left in no doubt that the kiss had been a 'one-off' happening and that she was unlikely ever to kiss him again.

He made no move to follow her but remained standing where he was in the Great Hall, which now seemed to have become so large and so empty that he did not clearly see the far end of it, nor the hammer beams overhead, nor even the near end where the gallery was, though perhaps he did not try to see any of these things, as he was thinking still of her and of what she had guessed he would do after he had retired from schoolmastering. He recognised that no matter how grim the effort to go on might be for him he could not escape his need to say to others the kind of things he had said to his class this morning, and that his need would animate his day-time thoughts and his dreams at night for as long as he was alive.

From a Seaside Notebook
(Nine Political Prose Pieces: 1976–1979)

1 The Juror

WALKED AGAIN yesterday afternoon along the asphalted cliff
path between Brandslow and Linbrook as I have done every
previous day of this windily-misty week. Only two years ago
I still didn't know that a strong east wind always goes up
over the heads of the walkers there after it has obliquely hit
the cliff-face on its way in from the open sea and before it
curves down to hurtle on inland – though it doesn't miss the
slightly higher heads of the hawthorns beside the path,
which have most of them become slopingly flattened out on
top. Herring-gulls were making use of the aerial upcurrent,
as I had noticed them doing earlier in the week, to glide
slowly against the wind and along yet high above the line of
the cliff-edge, gaining height as they glided, hundreds on
hundreds of them, far more than I'd seen before, momentarily sinister with their wings rigid-seeming like those
bombers in a mass air-raid; but soon I had the idea, in spite
of warning myself against indulging in anthropomorphic
sentiment, that they were behaving like this for enjoyment
rather than for any utilitarian predatory purpose. I wished I
was walking with some ornithologically knowledgeable
member of the local Natural History Society who could have
answered the no doubt elementary questions which were
coming into my mind about these gulls; and not long after

wishing this I saw, fifty yards ahead of me, a man of about my own age or possibly several years younger, certainly an Old Age Pensioner, who had come to a stop on the path and was watching the gulls just as I had been.

At first sight he gave more of a military than a nature-loving impression. He held his walking stick sloping up backwards under his arm like a sergeant-major carrying a swagger-stick on parade and his posture was noticeably upright, but something – perhaps merely his large-lensed steel-rimmed glasses – made me wonder whether he might be an intellectual; and he wore a riverside angler's hat (so I described it to myself) with a drooping brim all round it, the kind of hat I have at times thought I might like to wear, though I have always reverted quickly to the conviction that anything other than an ordinary flat cloth cap would give me a look of ostentation. I had an impulse to go up and speak to him but I was deterred by a return of my usual cautiousness, while I'm taking this favourite walk of mine along the cliff path, about getting into conversations with people who within three minutes or less would predictably reveal themselves as believing that young vandals should be birched, that militant trade-unionists should be sent to prison and that coloured immigrants should never have been allowed to settle in Britain. If I happened to catch the eye of this gull-watcher, I thought, I'd better confine myself to saying good afternoon or to exchanging joky comments about the weather, as with that cheery couple, a week before, the big broad man accompanied by a much smaller smiling woman and calling out to me as I passed them 'You've left the door open', meaning that the north wind was blowing violently from the path behind me into their faces, so that when we passed again half an hour later and I was walking against the wind while they had it behind them I was able to call out to them 'You haven't shut the door'. The gull-watcher, I suddenly saw, was making an interesting movement with his walking stick: he had brought it out from under his elbow and was lifting it quickly up with both his hands towards his right shoulder, like a sportsman about to fire a shot-gun. Perhaps the reason why he'd been staring at the gulls for so long was that he had been lost in a daydream of how many of them he could have brought down if only he had had a real shot-gun with him.

But I very soon admitted to myself that his taking hold of his stick with his left as well as his right hand and then tilting it up skywards was most probably due to there being no easier way for him to remove it from the awkward position in which he had been holding it under his arm. Why was I always so ready to suppose that if I got talking with anyone whom I said good afternoon to during my walks along this path I should be bound to find him or her full of reactionary opinions about everything? It was true that the majority of the walkers here – including the working-class ones, who anyway were usually indistinguishable from the fewer middle-class walkers in dress and appearance if not in their voices – were likely to hold such opinions, but no doubt they held them with varying degrees of conviction and as a rule unthinkingly. And if I assumed that nothing I or anyone else with an outlook similar to mine might say to them could alter theirs in the slightest then I would be no better than one of those intellectual renegades who have arrived at a philistine disbelief in the possibility of human progress. As for the gull-watcher, he looked like a man who might have interests out of the ordinary so my cautiousness about getting into conversation with him was perhaps not only socially reprehensible but might also be depriving me of a pleasure.

I began to move towards him; then I remembered an out-of-the-ordinary man I had once talked with at a point not much farther along this path than I had reached now. A man under fifty, hatless, slim, tall, with a sun-browned face and curly greying hair: the memory of him caused me to stop moving towards the gull-watcher and to pretend that my attention was caught by something out at sea. The hatless man had been walking along the middle of the path in the same direction as myself though more slowly, and as I had had to come rather close to him in order to get past him I had apologised, and this had given him the opportunity to start a conversation during which he had soon told me that he was a chartered accountant who had made money in South America and been able to retire early, that he had taken up nudism since retiring, that he liked lying naked on secluded parts of the cliffs, and that he and his wife normally went about in their house with no clothes on; then he had invited me to come along and join them any time, giving his address as 9 Melmare Avenue and his name as George Garstall, but I wasn't prepared to reveal even that my forename was Alan, far less that my surname was Sebrill and that I lived in St Aubyn's Street. When I had next come upon him walking along the same path I had avoided seeing him and every time after that he had reciprocally avoided seeing me. Not that I'm prejudiced against nudism – though when I tried it some years ago in winter with a group who met in a large London surburban house I singed myself slightly by standing with my back to a very hot coal fire – but I'm too old now to want to experiment with it again. I was still staring out to sea when I became aware that the man in the angler's hat was coming towards me, though with no evident intention of speaking to me. He did not look an importunate type. I decided to risk speaking to him.

I began lightly, in the tone of one walker commenting to another on the weather: 'All these gulls – they remind me of an air-raid'. Having said this I instantly feared he might think I was making an old-fashioned vulgar sea-side-

44

picture-postcard joke about the dangers from bird dropp-
ings, the sort of joke that would have invited him to add some
such remark as 'Thank God cows can't fly'. I quickly went
on: 'I wonder where they come from.' He took me seriously,
though there was a smile at the corners of his mouth. In a
non-middle class voice he said, 'They fly up from the
Council's refuse dump behind Linbrook.' Just in case he
might, if I gave him the chance, start volubly accusing the
Council of underspending on refuse disposal while over-
spending on education I at once told him that what puzzled
me most about the gulls was how they were able to glide
against the wind and to gain height at the same time. 'Many
kinds of large birds can do it,' he said. 'It's called dynamic
soaring. You could compare it to what yachts do when they
tack against the wind. Albatrosses can glide like that for as
much as a hundred miles sometimes.' I hadn't at all
expected him to be so knowledgeable. I asked with diffidence
whether the upcurrent of air from the cliff mightn't help the
gulls to gain height as they glided. He was a little doubtful
about this at first but when I pointed out that they seemed
nearly always to be following the line of the cliff-edge below
them as they soared, he soon said he thought I could be right.
I told him of my guess that they might be gliding just for
pleasure. The smile at the corners of his mouth became
larger. 'Perhaps,' he said. 'But it's all speculation. More
likely they're looking for food.' I admitted that my impression might be merely anthropomorphic, and I saw from
his look that he knew this word. I asked him whether he was
a member of the Natural History Society and he said he
wasn't. Seemingly guessing I was curious about how he had
acquired his aerodynamical knowledge, he explained, 'I
worked in the aircraft industry for a number of years.' He
went on to talk about the fauna (though he didn't use that
word) inhabiting the cliffs – rabbits, voles, kestrels, jack-

daws, sand martins and also house martins which were distinguishable from the sand ones by their white rumps – and about the differing effects that winds from different directions had on the stones and pebbles along the shore, sometimes piling these in a ridge against the cliff and sometimes scattering them all over the sands. I wish I'd listened to him more carefully and could remember now which winds had which effects. He said he'd got this information by talking with the longshoremen. All at once he asked me, 'What do you think were the happiest days of my life?' He paused, not for an answer from me but for effect, and long enough to enable me to imagine various answers he might give to his own question, such as 'when I was just mucking about in boats' or even 'when I was on safari in Africa'; but in actuality he told me, 'My happiest days were a fortnight I spent serving on a jury. It gave me so many interesting insights into human nature.'

2 *An Intruder at Night*

———

IT STANDS there new and alone against the dark blue nylon-velvet curtains of our sitting-room, and we cannot for more than a moment become oblivious, even when we turn our backs on it, of the threat that is dormant behind the glaze of its single monstrous oblong eye. Why did we choose to have it brought into our seaside home, this instrument of the enemy, this electronic Trojan horse shod with stainless-steel castors, this box full of hostile untruisms poised to spill out upon us at the pressing of a button in the evening when our minds are least likely to be well awake? Have we become addicts of technology for technology's sake, craving to see in true colour the imitation blood of lawbreakers who are gunned down at the end of almost every episode of the latest moronic crime-thriller series, or the real blood of the oppressed which the agents of the enemy are daily shedding (though that we shall seldom be shown)? Oh certainly the power is ours to activate this instrument or not, and its eye can never watch us or record what visitors we have, nor does its chitin-like plastic casing conceal, so far as we know, a bug that could listen to us. We are not compelled to view and hear its slanted news selectively pictured and so winsomely mouthed by zombie-voiced cosmeticised newscasters, or its sober-sounding political commentaries with their constant denigration of militant trade unionists, their condemnation of all violence as mindless except the violence of the capitalist state engaged in neo-colonial or civil repression, their fairness which gives equal publicity to racist and to anti-racist opinions. We are free to prevent such poison from flowing out into our room and to switch on only those programmes that do not tempt us to take a sledge hammer and wreck beyond repair this technological marvel we are paying so much money for, programmes of sport, of music, of dancing, of intentional farce and clowning, of drama, of painting and sculpture, of nature and of science, and also of social reality which the enemy is cunning enough to let us view sometimes though rarely, with the aim of persuading us how impartial all this televising is. But even the best of programmes like these will become dope for us if we have bought this box with the determination never to see the worst. We need to know what is being shown to those viewers who when they happen to watch the news do not begin to doubt they are seeing with their own eyes through the glass of this miracle window the world outside as it actually is. We and others who think like us need to say everything we can to expose, among as many of those viewers as we can reach, the enemy's televisionary distortion of reality which sooner or later reality itself will force them to recognise, and to recognise all the sooner for our trying to expose it but all the later if we do not try, however little effect what we say may seem to have on them at first. And when the awakening of the workers comes, and they assert themselves as at last they must if the human race is to survive, there may then be found among the newscasters and commentators some whose sympathies will be, perhaps always were, with them and not with the enemy, and who will look out and speak out from the glazed screen of the box one evening with the voices and the faces not of the zombies they never truly were but of living human beings.

3 *The Poet Who Died*

———

ON SUCH a morning, so warmly autumnal and so hazelessly blue, with the high small field ahead of me ending where 'the chalk wall falls to the foam' as he said of another cliff in his poem forty years ago about a summer island, I could almost more easily believe that he is looking down at this scene from the Christian heaven or up at it from the Christian hell than I can realise that everything I am glad to view from here, and would view in a poorer imaginative light if I did not know his poem, must remain everlastingly invisible to him now. But although I have to accept the truth that he cannot become conscious of any place or person again, I am free today of the grief I felt for many days after he died.

How unexpectable the depth of that grief seemed. Through the years since I had met him last only my dreams at night had imaged him as the friend he used to be when we were young, though his appearing in them more often than anyone else alive or dead should have made me aware how much I still loved him as a poet. So too should my excessive daytime resentment against his later political perversities: his calling the nineteen-thirties 'a low dishonest decade', intending these words as an attack not on the fascists or the appeasers of fascism but on the anti-fascists whose supporter and one of whose highest hopes ('clever hopes' in his own renegade phrase) he himself had recently been; his shallow little elegy praising the assassinated President Kennedy as 'a just man'; his reported approval of the war against Vietnamese peasants begun by Kennedy and continued by two successive Presidents and denounced by many other poets as its horror grew, until at last he said that a poet should not be required to express opinions on public events any more than a dustman should. If he had become an active anti-human politician instead of remaining a poet for whom art was essentially a supreme game and who may sometimes have played with social and political ideas in much the same way that he tried out unfamiliar words when he wrote his poems, the bitterness I felt could hardly have been keener. I ought to have recognised that my indignation was less against the injuriousness of his opinions than against him for holding them. I could not dissociate him from himself as the young poet who for me and for other poets of his generation had been the only potential giant among us. It was because of his younger self that when I, listening to the news as usual from a transistor radio at breakfast-time, first heard of his sudden death in Vienna, I felt the beginnings of a desolation which was to extend day by day until I came to think it might last for the rest of my life.

But the shadow cast by the older poet over the younger, emphasising the once venial-seeming faults that had prefigured some of the worst he developed later and diminishing the light of those earlier poems where his potential greatness had been clearest, was lessened when he died, and has disappeared this morning. His younger consciousness, hopeful of the world still, has been brought to life in my consciousness now by a scene much like the other which his poem of forty years ago recorded, and that is why I could almost believe he is invisibly here with me looking at this calm cliff-mirroring sea, these ships diverging on their

'urgent voluntary errands', this gull that 'lodges' (how exact
an image) 'a moment on its sheer side'.

4 *I Dreamt of a Valley*
(Creys-Malville, July 1977)

———

IT WAS as though I looked out from a place of shadow and saw in the sunlight a human crowd of thousands descending a wide green slope towards me, the foremost among them wearing motor-cycle crash-helmets and carrying sticks and home-made shields and with scarves or handkerchiefs or even what I thought might be Second World War gasmasks over their faces, but the majority were unarmed and seemed to have taken no self-protective precautions. They were dressed for summer and their colours were red, blue, white and green, in that order of frequency, like the colours of holiday visitors to a July beach on a hazily sunny afternoon when a low tide gives room along broad miles of sand for uncountable numbers, and the watcher from the cliff hears at intervals shrill happy cries rising above the constant stridulation of continuous human talk. Yet the crowd on the green slope were soundless, and I found this unnatural, especially as some of them appeared to be shouting.

Then a voice, no less unnatural, uncertainly located and expressionless and electronically amplified, coming perhaps from the shadows behind me but also simultaneously from the sunlit gap between the trees in front of me, said, 'These are the men and women of violence. They hold in contempt the institutions of our democratic society. They are leftists and foreigners. Let us honour the peace-keeping forces who risk serious injury to defend this prohibited zone from their assault.'

In the green shadowiness around me men darkly uniformed ran forward carrying guns muzzle-loaded with cylindrically-shaped tear-gas grenades which from kneeling positions they fired out soon into the sunlight. I watched the high smoke-trailing trajectory of these and their explosions down among the crowd and the white gas pluming up and spreading like a low fog that hid almost everyone at first except a few of the masked and crash-helmeted vanguard who advanced through it.

The voice said nothing about casualties, but I read in a newspaper afterwards that as well as the hundred or so demonstrators who had to be taken to hospital some riot-policemen were injured, among them four whose hands were blown off by prematurely exploding grenades and who had only been obeying orders, carrying out the will of a freely elected government and protecting this officially chosen site where the construction of a plutonium-burning fast breeder reactor would do so much to improve the health of the national economy.

5 *Love is Nice*

———

I NOTICED today that the re-glazed windows of the semi-circular shelter beside the cliff path had not been broken again yet, but the word 'shit' had been written in what looked like shit across the glass of two of them. I was less startled by this than by an inscription in black crayon I saw a few minutes afterwards on a concrete-covered bastion of the nineteenth-century fort which now encloses a tea garden – 'Love is nice', with the signature 'Caroline' in another handwriting below it.

I wondered if the author of it had been Caroline's seducer, who had persuaded her to sign it. Or might it be the title of a pop-song familiar to almost everyone fifty years younger than me? Or did it truly express the mutual feeling of two equal lovers, the calm and the bliss of their gratified desire, so different from the callous malevolence which too many of the old too often let themselves believe is general among teen-agers now? 'Oh Caroline,' I said to myself, 'I love you.'

A pale-haired young man in a fashionably faded blue denim jacket with buttoned breast pockets was standing a little farther along the path alone against the iron railings near the cliff edge, and staring out to sea. He could not be watching a high-powered motor-boat with its wake swelling up behind it, nor a yacht with a vividly striped spinnaker bosoming out in front, since no boats of any kind were visible at that moment in the bay. What held him there could only be the sea – more palely green, except where small slow-moving cloud shadows empurpled it, than his jacket was palely blue. But as I was thinking how ignorant the old are if they suppose that natural scenery has no appeal now to any of the young (who sometimes, it's true, walk vacant-eyed along this same path carrying loud transistor radios on their shoulders close to their ears) his hand moved automatically to one of his breast pockets from which he drew out a cigarette packet; then entranced still by the sea he slowly extracted the only remaining cigarette, and after a pause unconsciously dropped the empty packet on to the grass and the celandines near his feet.

I blamed myself, as I walked on past where he stood, for being disappointed and even indignant with him. My anger, I knew, should be turned against a class society which had conditioned him to behave in this way, and against the poisoners who profited commercially from the addiction of millions like him. As for the shit-writers and window-smashers who savaged the amenities enjoyed by Old Age Pensioners like me and had made me idealise Caroline for not being brutish like them, what was their offence compared with the crime of their powerful wrongers who had left them with little except destructiveness to live for? But I am mistaken, I thought, if I regard the violence of the young vandals of the capitalist world solely as a symptom of contemporary capitalism's general disease. What they do is also the beginning of a rebellion, blind now and futile and all too liable at worst to be misdirected even into racist murder, but capable at best of homing in eventually on the real enemy and of helping to bring revolutionary destruction to a system whose death is overdue. Love cannot bring this, and only through this can love come into its own.

6 We Call Them Grockles

———

NEAR THE end of the holiday season hundreds of visitors still were sitting in deck-chairs on the pavement when I walked along the esplanade one cloudless day, many of them looking at tabloid newspapers which they held up in front of their faces as if they wanted to avoid seeing the sea. And behind them, on the landward side of the road, were the gift shops, more even than there had been the previous year, each with an almost identical display of fancy goods in its show-windows – mainly ceramic or coloured cast-concrete figures and heads, highly glazed dark brown cart horses, faithful-eyed retrievers, grey cats green-eyed and long-necked like Modigliani women, faces of one-eyed pirates, of Red Indians, of Robin Hood, the fully clothed body of a homburg-hatted drunkard holding a bottle with both hands and lying happily in a bath, statuettes of Venus resembling off-white sugar and of bow-bellied Mr Pickwick senti-mentally beaming, and least cheaply priced of all a large china boot with its toe-cap wrenched up from the sole to show a redly illumined cave in which a family of rabbits squatted. But though I have never thought that commercial-ised popular art can do no harm at all to anyone, I did not feel a loathing for those objects in the show-windows as I did for the photographs and headlines of the tabloid newspapers, whose cumulative poison the holiday-makers were so comfortably drinking in.

Half way along the esplanade where steps go down to the beach and a row of bathing huts begins (every one of them with its own fancy name painted on it above the doorway, such as Cabana, Gayfere, Eureka and – facetiously cynical – Thisuldoem) I halted and leant on the red tubular railing that tops the sea-wall; and I looked across the sands, less crowded with holiday-makers than a fortnight before, towards the small tumbling waves and the unvarying line of the horizon. Soon, as if during a sea voyage a fellow passenger I had not yet talked with had come to stand next to me at the rail of the ship, I was aware that a longshoreman I had often seen before was close beside me; and when he spoke to me I knew he recognised I was not a visitor but a resident. 'Two more weeks and all the grockles will have gone,' he said.

My interest in words made me risk asking him whether he could tell me how this name had come to be used locally for visitors, and I added (in order to avoid giving any impression of blaming him for it or of wanting to convict him of ignorance), 'No one seems to know.' He admitted, 'to be quite honest', he hadn't given it a thought till now. Grockles they were and had been ever since he could remember, and the name suited them. It made him think of cockles crowded in a cockle-bed or of crockery broken into small bits sticking out of the sand. And they got worse every year, with their litter and their selfishness. There had been a time when they would have brought some of the deck-chairs back to his hut instead of leaving the lot for him to collect and carry before the tide came in. Last week one middle-aged couple had even wanted to bring their own chairs on to the beach and when he'd told them it was against Council regulations they had tried to argue that the charge was too high and that in any case the beach ought to be free – as if he himself didn't have to pay more money each year to the Council for the right to hire out chairs here. 'I hate them,' he said, meaning perhaps the Council as well as the grockles, though chiefly the grockles.

I would have laughed or smiled if I hadn't seen how serious he looked as he said it. Afterwards on my way up from the esplanade to the High Street I was thinking, 'He hates them because if he loved them he might have to despise himself for earning his living out of a relationship with them which must be primarily a cash and not a human one.' Then I realised how objectionable my own attitude to them had been during my walk along the sea front. Instead of being indignant against commercialised popular art I had let myself feel contemptuous of them for demanding the goods that the gift shops had sprung up in such numbers to supply, and more inexcusably still I had come near to despairing of their ever seeing through newspaper propaganda which flattered their prejudices and persuaded them to act against their own interests. I had forgotten that for me the alternative to believing in the eventual awakening of the people, and to doing what I can towards bringing this about, would be to hate and despise myself.

7 The Spectacle

A TANKER is on fire in the bay. No one has been killed or seriously injured, according to this morning's news, though the fire is said to have started with an explosion in the engine room when the ship ran aground on the sandbank. Black smoke turbulently congested rises heavily from the white superstructure close to the funnel at the ship's stern and does not seem to become any less black as gaining height it expands and is carried slowly off to the north-east by the prevailing wind, away from the shore and the houses of this seaside town. Watchers in or near the town wonder whether the fire may yet spread to the long foredeck beneath which most of the oil-tanks are. Flame infrequently gleams out of the smoke above the superstructure but is continuous along a line extending from the stern for at least a hundred yards backwards over the sea's surface. Dutch salvage tugs, sent for by the ship's owners or the insurers but not by the multi-national oil company whose oil is burning here and whose profits this accident will not decrease, have crossed the channel and are waiting around the tanker, while two fire-floats, one on each side of the stern, throw up arching jets of sea-water, mixed perhaps with chemicals manufactured by the same oil company, on to the invisible part of the super-structure where the smoke is densest. The best view of what will happen next is likely to be had by walkers along the cliff path, and many people from this town and from elsewhere for miles around are going up there now.

They are doing no harm, are not obstructing salvage operations as sightseers sometimes obstruct the rescuers at major air accidents. Yet the undisguised avidity of their interest shocks me, and I am ashamed to recognise that I am a sightseer too. A number of them have arrived with binocular cases slung over their shoulders, which I at least haven't, but this may be for no finer reason than that I lack the nerve to expose my curiosity so blatantly. What are they thinking while they watch the tanker burn? I doubt whether any of them (they are nearly all males, I notice) would go so far as to say to himself, as Lucretius says to his readers, how sweet it is to gaze from the land at another's struggles on the sea. Ancient Roman sentiments perhaps really were more shamelessly inhumane than the modern world's are even at present, though Lucretius did also say that other people's afflictions were not in themselves a source of delight to him, and he did hate war. Possibly most of the gazers up here on the cliff are altruistically hoping that the fire-floats will succeed in putting the fire out soon and that no one still on board will be injured and that the tugs will get the tanker off the sandbank without further accident. Others here may be watching with an anxious awareness of how unpleasant it would be for the inhabitants of the town if the wind were to change its direction and to blow the black smoke landwards, or if the oil slick trailing from the ship's stern were to stop burning and to drift intact on to the shore. But there may be a few whose sentiments are as bad as the worst that any Ancient Roman would have been capable of and who would enjoy nothing more than to see the tanker and the fire-floats and the tugs go up in one huge explosion. It's conceivable that such a disaster would supremely delight the football club supporter who wrote recently in green paint on the door of the municipal gardener's hut not far from the cliff path: P.F.C. kill 4 fun. And is there no schadenfreude in the mind of the thin tall old man who, bent-kneed and bent-shouldered, crosses the path with a spidery quickness towards the railing at the cliff edge and lifts to his eyes a large but light new pair of Japanese field-glasses?

I know I shall reproach myself later for pessimistic arrogance yet I cannot be confident now that anyone I see here feels as I do about this accident. I think there may be two or three who might blame the captain for his bad navigation, or even the ship-owners for cheaply employing someone insufficiently qualified, but they would hardly recognise the responsibility of the multi-national company or of the economic system which puts profits before human lives. Will they feel anger next time when an even larger tanker is wrecked in the bay and its oil floods out on to the beaches here? Would they protest if a ship carrying atomic waste were to sink here? Will they and others like them take action before the first live missile from a submerged nuclear submarine breaks the surface of the sea and goes on its arching way over the inhabited land?

8 *The Last Good Thing that a Bad Reporter Should Heed*

———

I WAS standing at a window in a seaside boarding house. I had written an article entitled 'The Last Good Thing that a Bad Reporter Should Heed'; and it had been published in a Victorian book with brown cloth covers, which was now lying on a table beside me. Events began to happen as if to illustrate this title. Something was falling out of the sky. At first I thought it was a huge aeroplane, but then I saw it was a section of a house with men standing on all the floors of its exposed interior. It fell slowly into the sea. I ran down to the shore, where I found a man whom I took to be a 'savage' and whose naked body was quite transparent like flexible glass. He was aiming a rifle at the men on the floors of the house, which was beginning to sink in the sea. I tried unsuccessfully to wrest the rifle from him. I did succeed in preventing him from firing it, but at the same time I guiltily felt that my prior duty was to save the men from drowning. This seemed to explain the title of my article.

Why did I think of him as a savage? I may for a moment have hoped to believe that he was an aboriginal anti-imperialist and that there was no need for me to do anything to help his enemies who were the occupants of the falling mansion. Yet all the while I really knew they were not imperialists but victims of imperialism in its long-drawn-out decline, and I suspected that he might be one of its agents disguised as an aborigine but giving himself away by the slick technological up-to-dateness of his flexible-glass physique. Why did I try to wrest the rifle from him instead of running as fast as I could down to the sea to take a boat out to the men who although some of them might get shot would all of them drown if I did not rescue them? My motivation became transparently clear to me as I began to wake out of my dream. I had been afraid that unless I could seize the rifle from the naked robot he would shoot me when he saw I meant to save the men. My will – like the will of many another 'reporter' (or imaginative writer) of my generation – to make the good cause of the anti-imperialist stuggle my first concern had been flexible; and by grappling with a lesser danger, which was also a more immediate one to myself, I had hoped I would partly justify my failure to do anything against the greater. No wonder my article with its timidly cryptic title had found a publisher in an age notable for hypocrisy. Just before I became quite fully awake from my dream I wished that the book on the table had not been a Victorian one with brown cloth covers but a modern paperback which had included a serious essay by me entitled 'The First Bad Thing That a Good Reporter Should Heed'.

9 *Do Others*

───────

AN HOUR ago, in this seaside holiday town where I used to be brought as a child by my mother every August, I saw coming towards me along the esplanade a boy aged four or five wearing a white T-shirt with a slogan printed on it in blue capital letters: DO OTHERS BEFORE THEY DO YOU. He passed close to me, but because I was still staring at those words to make sure I hadn't misread them I had no time to see the faces of the adult couple walking beside him who were likely to be his parents; and although very soon after they had gone by me I turned to look back, and his small white T-shirt helped me to identify him among the moving crowd on the pavement behind me, I could not distinguish which adults he was with. I wish now more and more that I had followed them; yet, if I had, how much would their faces or their voices have revealed to me about what had been going on in either of their minds the day they had walked into that Mini-Market – it used to be called 'the arcade' in my childhood – at the western end of the esplanade, and coming up to the counter where many already printed T-shirts are displayed together with a large notice saying *Shirts printed while-u-wait*, the father or the mother had asked the wearied young assistant to print on a child-size shirt the words I read today?

My guess was almost certainly wrong that a slogan so dismissively parodying the New Testament precept 'Whatsoever ye would that men should do to you, do ye even so to them' had not been on show in the Mini-Market when the mother and father had arrived there, and that they were unusual people who had read it in Dickens's *Martin Chuzzlewit* or might even have thought it up themselves. One or two of the mottoes and captions I took note of when I looked in there earlier this season were hardly less anti-social, as for instance *'Sworn to fun and loyal to none'*, which the assistant told me was a favourite with motor-cycling groups. (I couldn't clearly make out the details of the sepia-coloured design below that inscription, but I seemed to see a smudgily pictured naked human pair semi-recumbently facing yet leaning backwards from each other like the figures of Neptune and the earth goddess on the golden salt cellar made by Benvenuto Cellini, and a second pair airborne above them embracing like the personified winds in Botticelli's *Birth of Venus*, and higher still a fan-shaped arrangement of sharply pointed wings – whether feathered or webbed I couldn't be sure – attached to indistinct bodies of angels or of devils.) The words and designs on the shirts for children had a narrower philosophical significance perhaps, though some of them were equally cynical: *Kid for Sale* was the caption beneath a luridly coloured caricature of a howling toddler, and *Mark – little stinker* was illustrated by an animal of no recognisable species atrociously drawn in the act of discharging a stone from a catapult, and even the apparently innocent *My Nanny loves me* could have been intended to imply that only the grandmother loved the child. DO OTHERS BEFORE THEY DO YOU may well have been one of the slogans that the parents I failed to identify an hour ago had found already printed on shirts for sale in the Mini-Market, and they may have chosen it simply because it amused them, or more seriously because they hoped it might encourage their boy to stand up for himself against attackers at school, or they may just have wanted a shirt with words across its front, no matter which words. But my curiosity on the esplanade and afterwards about whether they had thought of the slogan themselves or not has become less keen now than another feeling I began to have at the same time there: I am disturbed that words so assertively expressive of the real ethos of capitalism should have been flaunted across a T-shirt bought for a child by parents who, like the majority of summer visitors here nowadays, were most probably working-class.

Are capitalist principles so generally accepted in these times by the workers that our rulers need no longer try to hide the predatoriness of their system under a smoke-screen provided by the preachers of Christian love? Certainly the five chapels and the three churches which were in this town when I was a child are still here as buildings, but the congregations except at the Catholic church are small, in spite of promotional activities such as weekly Bright Hours for the elderly; and one of the chapels has been converted into a workshop for the repair of television sets, and the Congregational chapel I was taken to on Sunday mornings by my Anglican mother to please my grandparents has to share a minister now with another chapel in a neighbouring town. If I were to meet him I expect I would find him just as sincere as the Congregational minister here in my childhood, Mr Bynner, who impressed me by praying aloud without book, seemingly trusting to inspiration for the words he so unhesitantly spoke as he stood on the platform behind a polished wooden railing that reminded me of the balustrade of a staircase, while at his back an undecorated concave end-wall distempered in pale blue helped to concentrate the attention of the congregation upon him, and directly in front

66

of him was an unpretentious table on which (though not every Sunday) I saw what looked like an expanded domestic cruet holding many small hygienically separate glasses with Communion wine in each of them. Our rulers may even have come to sense a danger to them in Christian love – especially when the Churches, with an eye no doubt partly to their own survival after the final defeat of imperialism, overlook Christ's teaching about rendering unto Caesar the things that are Caesar's and give material support to Third World peoples who have taken up arms against colonial oppression. And yet the capitalists must feel a need – as their failed resort to fascism in Italy and Germany has already shown – for an idealistic ideology which could hold the minds of the people no less strongly than religion once could, and they must be aware that frankly stated primitive capitalist principles like DO OTHERS BEFORE THEY DO YOU cannot be expected to appeal even to the least politically awake among the workers for ever.

Let me be as constant in my hope as our rulers should be in their fear that a time will come when most of the workers will recognise behind all such divisive slogans an intention which is hostile to them, and when the words PEOPLE BEFORE PROFITS will sometimes be seen in letters of red on the white T-shirts of parents walking with their children along the esplanade here in August.

Over the Cliff

THE GRANDFATHER pointed out almost immediately after he had sat down next to the grandmother on the seat in the woods that as much of the sky as they could get a clear view of through the gap between trees in front of them was uninfested by military aircraft, and that the wider sea far below them had no nuclear submarines visibly patrolling it. 'Isn't this typical of him?' the grandmother complained half-jokingly to their daughter and son-in-law who were sitting the other side of her. 'Take him anywhere beautiful and if there's the least blot on the landscape it's usually the first thing he'll call attention to, and now he has to remind us of blots that aren't here.' They all laughed, the grandfather too – though not the grandsons, who were bright enough to have been amused if they'd heard what she'd said, but both of them had run ahead farther into the woods to look for clematis 'lianas', as they called them, which hung like long hard ropes from the branches of high trees and could be used for swinging on across minor chasms between the mossed rocks beneath. He was thinking of saying something to defend himself, such as 'The more beautiful a place is the more it ought to alert us to the things that threaten it', when he and the three others as well heard an interesting sound, a rapid and resonant high-pitched tapping or drumming, which came from far-off in the woods.

'A woodpecker,' the son-in-law said. The sound stopped, and all four of them sat staring into the trees towards where it had come from. After quite a long interval they heard it again. The grandfather thought that its rhythm made it seem almost like the noise of distant machine-gun fire; then he told himself that in thinking this he was being as crudely insensitive as if he'd likened the April leaf-buds opening so numerously on the branches above him to the rash of a skin disease. When the sound stopped once more he and the others sat back and relaxed instead of concentrating on listening for it to be repeated, and they looked downwards through the gap between the trees in front of them at the green and hummocky stretch of land that descended to the edge of the invisible cliff and to the morning sheen on the calm sea beyond.

'This really is a lovely place,' the son-in-law said.

'Even the seat we're sitting on is lovely,' the daughter said. 'Look at the decorative ironwork at the end there. The detail may be a bit clogged up with all the coats of paint it's had since Queen Victoria's day, but unornamented modern seats in public places are bleak compared with this one.'

'And this one hasn't been made so high that little old ladies and even average-sized women couldn't sit on it without having to dangle their legs in the air,' the grand-mother said. 'Most seats nowadays seem to have been designed for male-sized legs only.'

The grandfather refrained from saying, 'And another thing that's lovely about this seat is that it hasn't been vandalised yet,' though he knew his saying so would not have spoilt the pleasure it gave the others, any more than his reminding them earlier on of military aircraft and nuclear submarines had poisoned their view of the sky and the sea. They had been right to laugh at him then, he thought. For some months past he had been allowing himself to become increasingly pessimistic, had seen only the blots on the landscape, and his awareness that the profit-seekers and the polluters and the militarists possessed the means of destroying the human race had been more constant than his belief that the people of the world would rise to defeat them before it was too late. The belief revived in him now. As he sat under the trees and looked towards the sea he had a feeling of exaltation and of hope such as he had only rarely had during recent years. And he knew from former experience that though a mood of this kind was not likely to persist in its present intensity for more than an hour at most, or possibly not even for more than a few minutes, its effect on his general outlook would be long-lasting.

Perhaps it was going to be interrupted now. A tall lean-legged man in khaki shorts came walking moderately fast down the narrow path to the seat. He hesitated, and then stopped to ask whether a little boy had passed this way.

'He's wearing an army-style dark green pullover with imitation suede shoulder patches. He has curly hair. He's six.'

'I'm afraid we've not seen him,' the son-in-law said. 'Did you come through these woods before you missed him?'

'No, we missed him on our way here. I thought there was just a chance he might have run off here in front of us without our noticing, but as you haven't seen him I suppose he didn't. Now I'd better go and join one of our girls who is looking for him in the opposite direction.'

The man spoke in the tone of someone thinking aloud rather than addressing anyone else. He turned to walk away.

'Well, good luck,' the son-in-law said.

'He may have gone back to the hotel we're staying at. It's quite near, and he knows how to get there.' The man gave a brief smile which he tried to make unanxious; then he went away up the path more quickly than he had come down it.

Soon after he was out of hearing the grandfather said, 'He's obviously the boy's father. At first I thought he might be a scoutmaster looking for a strayed member of his cub-pack.'

'I felt we ought to offer to help in some way,' the daughter said.

'I did too,' the son-in-law said. 'That's why I asked whether he had come through here before missing the boy. If he'd told us he had I could have offered to go with our lads to search around in the woods – though that might have sounded rather alarmist perhaps.'

'The boy is six and knows how to get to the hotel, and he may simply have felt he would like to go off on his own for a while,' the grandmother said. 'He may not be lost at all, as far as he's concerned.'

The son-in-law said, 'We might be able to help on our way back if he's still not been found by then.'

'Yes,' the daughter said. 'And we could start walking back now.'

'I'll go and fetch the lads,' the son-in-law said.

He went up the path and at the top of it he stood still to look ahead into the woods, but apparently he couldn't see either of the grandsons. He called out their names, and got no answer. He came back to the seat.

'They're hiding,' he said. 'They're going to track us when we move off.'

Three years before he had led them in crawling as undetectably as possible through the undergrowth of these same woods and making quick dashes between concealing boulders beside the path which their mother and grand-parents were walking along ahead of them, and each year since then the boys had repeated this game without their father who became one of the tracked instead of being the leading tracker.

'We oughtn't to keep them waiting any longer perhaps,' the grandfather said. Hearing about the missing boy had predisposed him to feel a slight anxiety about them. He got up and began moving away from the seat, and the others came with him.

Every now and then, as they walked along the winding and switchbacking path among ash-trees and sycamores and beeches, they would look back and try to glimpse – though hoping to avoid being seen to see – some revealing disturbance of the undergrowth, or possibly only the blobby green and brown army-style camouflage pattern on the floppy-brimmed hat worn by the younger grandson. But they reached the end of the woods without having detected any such signs.

They came out into the open. To their left the short-grassed ground, not hummocky here, sloped only gently downwards towards the cliff-edge, and to their right it did not rise much until it met the base of a perpendicular inland cliff from the upper part of which there were sharply-defined horizontal strata jutting out. Nothing near the path on either side could give cover for trackers. After walking along it for a short while the son-in-law and then the other three stopped to look back towards the woods.

'They aren't following us,' the son-in-law said. 'I'll go and see what they're up to.'

The others stood waiting on the path when he had gone. The grandfather became a little more anxious, though he told himself that this was unreasonable. After all, the younger grandson was no longer a six-year-old and the elder would soon be in his teens. As for the clematis lianas, they had been strong enough to bear the grandfather's own weight when he had tested one or two of them a few years before. But tree-climbing, which the grandsons enjoyed even more than swinging on lianas, could look more dangerous sometimes. In these woods there was one tree they were especially fond of getting up into, an oak, not very high in itself but perched on top of a huge sheer-faced boulder and gripping this with roots that reached down from its thick trunk like talons from the leg of some giant bird such as the Roc of the Arabian Nights: to fall from a branch of this tree would more probably than not be fatal. But the grandsons were careful climbers, having been taught by the son-in-law never to move more than one limb at a time as they climbed. In any case, if there had been an accident now it would have been unlikely to have involved them both equally, and one of them would have been able at least to call for help. The grandmother and the daughter, as they stood waiting on the path, showed no uneasiness, nor did they feel any. And within five minutes the son-in-law came walking back out of the woods with the two grandsons.

'What happened to you?' the daughter asked the boys.

'We thought you were going to walk on and you would come up with us,' the elder grandson said, unapologetic and unaggrieved.

'We saw a green woodpecker,' the younger said. 'It went into a hole in a pine tree.'

'The hole was very narrow, and the woodpecker looked very big,' the elder said. 'We couldn't think how it would be able to turn round inside the hole and come out head first.'

'And did it turn round?' the grandfather asked.

'No, it came out backwards,' the younger said.

'Tail-first,' the elder said, 'and it flew away so quickly that we didn't see it turn round even when it took off.'

The six of them, bunching rather closely together, walked slowly on along the not very broad path. Ahead of them and to the right of the path there was a thickly-growing clump of blackthorn trees, with the white tips of buds beginning to show on the twigs. The grandfather said:

'I once knew a cricket-club groundsman who when there was a cold wind at the beginning of May used to say that in Kent, where he was born, it was called the blackthorn hatch.'

Immediately after they had passed the blackthorn trees they came upon a group of four people, who had been hidden from them till now by these trees, – a man and a woman and two teen-age girls, the man and the girls standing up and the woman sitting on a seat like the one in the woods. The man was the same who had been searching for the little boy. The son-in-law spoke to him:

'Have you had any luck?'

'Not yet,' the man said. 'I've just been down to the hotel and there was no sign of him there.' He sounded a little out of breath. 'One of the girls has been to the beach and she was told he had been seen running along it earlier on, but she couldn't find him.'

The mother's face, large-browed and handsome, had a fixed look of anxiety, and there was blankness on the faces of the two girls. The group seemed to be undecided what to do next. There was a silence.

The son-in-law said:

'We'll keep our eyes open for any sign of him as we walk on.'

'Thanks,' the man said, almost expressionlessly.

The son-in-law and the other five of his group moved off quite quickly, not sorry that his offer to watch out for the boy gave them an opportunity to escape from the embarrassment of staying any longer unhelpfully with the distressed four.

After they had been walking on for several minutes along the path, and the daughter had answered some of the grandsons' questions to her about the boy, there was an explosion, crashingly loud and seeming very near. The grandfather briefly thought it could be from gunnery practice at sea or from a fighter plane breaking the sound-barrier, but then there was a second explosion, not followed by a third, and he knew what he had really heard.

'Maroons,' he said. 'Someone has gone over the cliff.' He saw the shock on the faces of the grandsons, and he added, 'Whoever it is won't have fallen all the way down to the bottom. Otherwise there would have been no need to call out the cliff-rescue team, which is what the maroons will do. Someone might have been trying to climb up the cliff, and have got stuck half way. It often happens.'

They had all come to a stop on the path, with the same thought in all their minds. They looked towards the inland cliff and along the steep face of it that was uninterruptedly viewable for a considerable distance both to the left and to the right. None of them detected anything to indicate an accident. On the other side of the path the cliff that rose from the beach couldn't be seen by them except for its edge which here and there was unobscured by the wind-flattened branches of cliff-top hawthorn trees. The six began to walk on again. The grandfather was unable to reason himself out of a dreadful certainty quickly growing in his mind that the little boy must have tried to climb down this cliff and been killed. He thought of how the parents would feel, of how he would have felt in their place. He was sure that not even the firmest belief in a future for the human race on an earth free from disease and starvation and oppression and war would have given him any consolation for such a loss.

Within a few minutes he and the other five heard and then saw a helicopter approaching over the sea. Its colour was naval grey, though with a band of vermilion round part of its fuselage, and for a moment the grandfather thought of the military gunship helicopters that had been used to shoot down villagers in Vietnam. It flew up to the cliff several hundred yards ahead of them and only a few feet higher than the edge, did not pause at all, turned through a half-circle and flew out to sea again, quite far, before turning towards the same place on the cliff once more and then once more flying out to sea. They soon came to where the path they were on met a narrower path which sloped downwards from it in the direction of the beach and alongside the cliff-face. 'This isn't too steep for you, is it?' the son-in-law asked the grandmother, and she said that it wasn't. She didn't need to ask why he had decided to follow this path instead of continuing along the other which would have got them home sooner, and the grandfather refrained from suggesting to him that perhaps it might be better for the grandsons not to be taken where they might see something horrible which they would never afterwards forget.

The helicopter approached the cliff a third time just before they all began going down the narrow path to the beach. This time it did not fly away but hovered above the cliff-edge. For a while the cliff hid it from them as they went down, and the grandfather was surprised by its nearness when he saw it again. In the past he had more than once seen rufous-winged kestrels hovering at this same spot – they were said to nest in the disused drainpipes protruding from the cliff-face here – and the flickering movement of the rotors of the noisy helicopter seemed to have some likeness to the quivering of the wings of a silently hovering kestrel. But the movement of the more rapidly revolving torque-counter-acting tail rotor did away with the likeness. The helicopter was not a raptor, nor a gunship. It was here to rescue someone, and the crowd on the sandy beach to which the son-in-law and the other five now came down were here to watch. Another crowd were at the top of the cliff, close-packed in a long single line behind the railing that guarded the cliff-edge; they were like theatre spectators looking downwards from a gallery in the sky. All at once from behind a thick bush only a quarter of the way down the cliff-face a man wearing a protective helmet rose into view in a standing position and holding on to a thin cable, now visible for the first time to the grandfather, which led up to the helicopter directly above; and in a sitting posture immediately below the man there was someone else of whom the grandfather could see little except the thin legs dangling out from the rescue strop. The helicopter swung away towards the sands, its transparent nose revealing the pilot at the controls: then it slowly descended and as it did so the two figures at the end of the cable were winched up to the open door in the fuselage. The grandfather was unable to see the helicopter after it touched down on the sands beyond the crowd, but his glimpse of the dangling legs, very thin and rather long, remained vividly in his mind.

The elder grandson said, 'It was a girl.' Until now neither of the grandsons had said anything since they had heard the maroons.

'Yes, I think it was,' the grandfather said.

The crowd in front moved forward a little, then stopped. The helicopter, which had been quieter after landing on the beach, became louder again, and rising up soon over the heads of the crowd it moved briefly sideways like an aerial crab towards the sea before it went off on a straight course parallel with the shore. The crowd began to disperse. The son-in-law spoke to a man who was passing close by him:

'Could you tell us what happened?'

'She is being taken to hospital,' the man said. His tone suggested that this was the end of the matter as far as his interest in it was concerned. He walked on.

The son-in-law and the other five turned and began to go back towards the path they had come down. The grand-father looked up at the cliff again. Poor girl, he thought, her fall could hardly have been an accident. How could she have got to the edge of the cliff without climbing over the railing there? And probably it was no accident that she had fallen at one of the few spots here along the cliff where there were thick bushes not far below the edge, and these seemed to be willows, not the spiny gorse that was more usual on the cliff-face.

'There's the boy,' the younger grandson suddenly said.

They all saw, coming in their direction and a hundred yards ahead of them, the tall man in khaki shorts whom they had met with his wife and his two girls on the cliff not long before, and walking beside him now there was a small boy wearing an army-style pullover. The two of them turned towards the cliff and began to go up the path alongside the cliff-face. For a moment or two the grandfather had a feeling of great relief and gladness, but he soon remembered the girl who was being flown to hospital. The helicopter was still clearly visible, flying not very high above the sea, and he could even see the grey and the vermilion on its fuselage. The killer grey of a nuclear-weaponed navy and the vermilion of life, he thought. He said to the grandmother:

'I was so glad about the boy that I almost forgot about the girl.'

'Yes, I felt the same,' she said. 'I suppose it was because we know she has been rescued, and we assume that the hospital will do all it can for her.'

The grandmother and grandfather were lagging behind the other four, but he noticed that the grandsons, who had spoken so little for the last quarter of an hour, were now talking freely with their parents, no doubt about the rescue, and he didn't quicken his walk in case their talk might be interrupted if he and the grandmother caught up with them at once. And there was something further he wanted to say to her.

'I've not become pessimistic about the future of the

human race, in spite of my habit of seeing the blots on the landscape,' he told her, 'but I do realise that even when all helicopters are used only for peaceful purposes and there's no more war anywhere there will still be accidental deaths, however rare, and the grief they will cause won't be any less than they cause at present – or it may be deeper because it will be more unexpected.'

'If we didn't realise that, we would be Utopians of the naïvest kind,' she said. 'And anyway how can we be sure the human race will have a future at all?'

'I don't think it's Utopian to believe that the peoples of the world will prevent the warmakers from annihilating them.'

'We can't be certain the peoples will take action soon enough.'

'If we're not to slacken in our opposition to nuclear weapons we'd better have faith that their use can be prevented, even though we've no certainty that it will be,' he said.

The grandsons and their parents had stopped at the bottom of the path that led up alongside the cliff-face to the top of the cliff, and they waited till the grandparents joined them again. When the family party began to go up the path, the grandsons in front and the parents next and the grandfather following the grandmother at the rear, the grandfather thought how strange it was that she who was temperamentally so cheerful should be unoptimistic about humanity's future, whereas he who tended to be pessimistic almost by nature was so hopeful about it theoretically.

The Interview

ONE SPRINGTIME Saturday afternoon Miriam Faulder was driving her car along a country road towards the weekend manor-house home of a cabinet minister who had recently said he wouldn't hesitate to press the nuclear button in response to a successful conventional attack by the Russians. 'Today I'm only going to reconnoitre,' she several times reassuringly reminded herself, though she knew she might just possibly be spotted and warned off even if she attempted little more than an exploratory stroll round the outside of the peripheral hedge or iron railings or broken-glass-topped wall or whatever might be there to exclude the public from the manor-house grounds. Her idea of eventually getting into the house itself, to see the minister and interview him for the bi-monthly magazine of the Linbrook nuclear disarmament group, could turn out at the very start to be as ludicrously impracticable as her fellow members on the editorial committee had probably thought it was when she had told them of it. But unlikelier things had been achieved by other peace campaigners elsewhere, for instance by the women who had climbed over the high wire fence of a foreign airbase in Britain to dance on the mounds above the silos where Cruise missiles were soon due to be placed; and how helpful she could be to the whole movement against the nuclear arms race if she were able to reveal something of what was really in the mind of this intellectually able politician who surely must know, unless he was clinically insane, that his declared willingness to press the button 'in defence of British freedom' was totally irrational.

She had never driven along this road before, nor seen the manor-house, although it was within five miles of Linbrook where she had lived with her husband and children for more than a year. She got a sudden first view of it as the car was beginning to go downhill after rounding a bend in the road. It was startlingly near. Behind the wrought-iron entrance gates a short straight driveway led towards a projecting central porch which together with two larger projecting wings on either side gave an 'E' shape to the face of the building, and no one could go by outside the gates – let alone walk up the driveway – with any assurance of not being seen from one or more of the many front windows. She soon reached a group of modern-looking farm buildings that were no doubt part of the manor estate, and the road she was driving along went directly ahead towards the house. The stone wall flanking the entrance gates was a low one, too low to hide the car from the house, so she decided to drive at a pace that would suggest she had no intention of stopping anywhere near here; but after passing the gates she felt she might have been going conspicuously fast, and she was relieved when not much farther on she came to a small church which she thought she could stop outside without attracting much attention. She would walk into the church-yard as if she were just a visitor interested in old churches.

She stopped her car in front of the lych gate. She saw no one around when she went in through the gate. The side of the churchyard nearest to the manor-house had a high dark hedge all the way along it, perhaps to ensure that the gravestones wouldn't be viewable from the windows of the house. Presumably at one time a rector of this parish would have owed his 'preferment' here to the lord of the manor in whose gift the 'living' would have been, and for all she knew of more recent ecclesiastical history, this cabinet minister who was the present owner of the manor estate might still have the right to choose an incumbent likely to be gratefully serviceable to him. The church porch she was walking towards faced the hedge-hidden house not the road. A path at right angles to the one she was on led straight from the porch to a narrow rectangular opening, like a bright doorway, in the lower part of the hedge. Across the opening there was a small white gate through which the lord of the manor and his family would have had easy access to the church without having to go along the road. She looked into the porch and saw that the heavy wooden door of the church was slightly ajar, though not sufficiently so for anyone inside to get a glimpse of her; then she turned away and walked quickly along the short path leading to the rectangular opening in the hedge. As she approached the white gate she had a view of a sunlit lawn and to the right of this a tree – *ceanothus* she guessed it might be – with spikes of deep blue blossom on it so amazingly profuse that she did not at first notice the man who was standing beneath it and looking down towards the soil round the base of its bole. He was heavy-shouldered, narrow-waisted and short-legged and had closely curly dark red hair. Like a bison, she soon afterwards thought. She immediately knew he was the minister. Without premeditation she opened the gate, attempting to lift the latch noiselessly, and went on to the lawn.

He heard the latch click and he turned towards her. His face with its broad-nostrilled nose and heavy-lidded eyes seemed huge, larger than in any of the newspaper photographs or television pictures she had seen of him. She spoke to him when she was at least ten yards away from him.

'My name is Miriam Faulder. I wrote to you at the ministry.'

From somewhere behind her a man she had been unaware of till this moment came up abruptly to place himself in front of her. His face had a disagreeably worried look. The minister called out to him:

'It's all right, Frooms.' (Or that was the name she thought she heard the minister speak.) 'You can leave this to me.'

Frooms stepped aside. The minister said to her:

'I know. I've been thinking of answering your letter. I hope you had an acknowledgment of it from the ministry.'

'Yes, thank you, I did. A month ago.'

He looked her up and down as she stood there in her light spring-time dress. Just possibly he might be ocularly frisking her for a concealed knife, or he might be superciliously putting her in her place because her saying 'A month ago' had seemed to criticise him for not having answered her letter yet, or – she doubtingly suspected – he might be showing a frank interest in the shape of her body.

'Well, since you're here,' he said, 'you'd better come into the house.'

He began to walk towards it, not waiting for her. She followed him, without trying to catch up with him. 'A wolf in bison's clothing,' she said to herself, and the phrase slightly pleased her until she had the thought that although he probably wasn't a wolf in a sexual sense he certainly was one in the ancient Roman sense of being capable of inhumanity towards his fellow human beings.

He did not once glance back at her during the time he took to cross the lawn and to reach a door near the corner of the house. His movement was brisk but a little stiff, not youthful: he couldn't be far off sixty. She pretended to be unaware that someone – Frooms she supposed – was following them both, and was rather closer to her than she had yet got to the minister who now opened the door and waited for her, still not glancing at her; then before she could come up to him, he moved on into the house, leaving her to shut the door if she chose, and she did shut it, hoping to do so in the face of Frooms whom she still pretended not to have noticed behind her.

She came into a low-ceilinged stone-floored room empty except for what she took to be an old butter churn, a barrel placed horizontally between iron supports with a crank handle at one end of it. The room was not much broader than the dark passage it led into through a doorless archway. Ahead of her the minister paused at the bottom of a stone stairway, and this time he did look briefly back, perhaps to make sure she had seen he was turning aside from the shadowiness of the passage to go up the stairs. As she reached the foot of the stairs she wasn't certain whether or not she heard someone open and shut the outer door through which she had entered the house. She followed the minister up the curving and brightening stairway to a carpeted passage broader and lighter than the stone-flagged one they had ascended from, and she found herself quite close behind him, not because his movement had become any less brisk as he'd climbed the stairs but because he had come to a stop now. From the far end of the carpeted passage a woman was approaching – tall, strongly-built, elaborately hairdressed, her face heavy-featured and morose yet handsome. Like an ex-wardress from a women's prison, Miriam imagined. Suppose on the pretext that Miriam might be a terrorist he were to order Frooms to help this woman overpower and forcibly body-search her while he would secretly or even openly watch them do it. An ambitious politician capable of public wickedness on a vast scale wouldn't necessarily be prudent enough to resist a liking he might have for indulging in repulsively sadistic private vice. Or perhaps he would order her to be searched for no other reason than that he genuinely suspected her of being a terrorist, and he wouldn't deign to stay and watch. But in actuality the woman stopped within a few yards of him, then turned round to walk back away from him, as if he had given her a sign that Miriam had been unable to see. He moved on to open a door at the side of the passage, and looking Miriam fully in the face now he raised his hand in a gesture of deliberate politeness to invite her to precede him into the room there.

She saw high shelves with books in them along the walls and between the windows. As he closed the door behind her she felt a tenseness that was only a little relieved when he came up beside her and pointed to an armchair for her to sit in. The chair was noticeably comfortable and its shape made any other position than sitting back in it – which she was determined to avoid – difficult for her. It was placed to the right of a broad fireplace that was half-hidden by a Victorian-seeming embroidered screen, and she got a quick impression that most of the furnishings around the room, including the chair she was trying to sit upright on, were Victorian also not Elizabethan or Jacobean, nor even eighteenth century like the decor and furniture of the only restored manor-house she had previously seen the interior of. The minister went over to a similar armchair at the other side of the fireplace. He sat down not in it but on one of its comfortably upholstered arms, dangling his short legs over this. He was purposely adopting a posture of casual superiority, she thought.

'I believe that in your letter to me you asked to interview me for a magazine you are helping to edit,' he said. So he hadn't personally read her letter, she assumed, or if he had he wasn't going to admit he had.

'Yes,' she said.

He stared at her. There was nothing bison-like about his face, though it still appeared huge, and his heavy-lidded eyes were abnormally prominent. He waited for several seconds, staring at her, before going on to ask, 'Has it occurred to you to wonder why I am willing to talk to you?'

She decided to ignore his question, which seemed meant to humiliate her.

'I didn't expect to have the chance of interviewing you today,' she said. 'I have come without my notebook.'

'That's just as well. Perhaps I shall feel able to speak more freely.' His tone was enigmatically ironic. 'You said in your letter that you wanted to know what could really be going on in the mind of a minister who had publicly declared himself in favour of a first strike with nuclear weapons if the circumstances warranted it.' He was quoting her word for word, so he must have personally read her letter. 'You distinguished yourself from other writers of nuclear disarmament letters to me by showing such an interest in my state of mind. I'll pay you the compliment of assuming you have enough imagination to realise that quite a large number of members of the public write to me, and that I can't spare the time to answer them personally or even to read the letters of most of them. The reason I'm talking to you now is that I'm interested in *your* state of mind – by which I mean the state of mind of all you younger disarmers, not just yours individually – and I get the impression from your letter than you could tell me what I want to know.'

The suspicion this brought instantly into her mind may have shown in her face.

'I'm not trying to recruit you as a spy,' he said.

She stared at him and he went on, 'I'm not curious about names or plans for future activities. But I am curious about what makes you – and other comfortably-off middle-class young married mothers in your movement – behave as you do.'

She would have asked him straight out how he had discovered she was married and a mother, but he continued without a pause.

'It's the absurd resilience of people like you that puzzles me. Haven't you read any history at all? Don't you know that the kind of thing you are trying to do has been tried innumerable times before and has always failed?'

'It couldn't have been tried until after President Truman ordered that the bombs should be dropped on Hiroshima and Nagasaki in 1945,' she said. 'And if you are suggesting that the campaign for nuclear disarmament totally failed in the 1960s, this isn't true. CND may have seemed to become dormant for a while then, but it has risen again more strongly than ever.'

'I'm not talking merely about CND. I'm talking about the propensity of a minority of men – and some women too – during the last three hundred years or so to believe in the perfectibility of the human race and the possibility of changing the world.'

'I don't believe in the perfectibility of the human race,' she said. 'I'm only concerned to do what I can towards abolishing nuclear weapons which will destroy the world unless they are abolished.'

'*Only.*' He echoed her word with restrained exasperation. 'Don't you understand that you and your associates could threaten the fundamental interests of the state in a way that no parliamentary party ever will? You may have been taught Marxism at your university, but you are certainly not a Marxist.'

She asked him straight out, 'How did you know I was at a university?'

'It's a reasonable assumption from your manner of writing. And I'm not wholly ignorant of the kind of teaching that goes on in our schools and colleges nowadays. But you seem too naïve to be a Marxist.'

'Are you implying I'm the dupe of Marxists?'

'No. I am not the sort of politician who pretends to believe that CND is run by Soviet agents, or by Marxists, and still less am I the sort who is paranoid enough actually to believe it. I know that real Marxists are only too pleased when a single-issue campaign like yours which is in line with their own policies springs up spontaneously under independent leadership. They will give you their full support of course, but far from wanting to dominate or use you or to turn your organisation into a socialist one – as the more sectarian leftist groups unintelligently try to do – they will let you use them, though naturally they'll hope that their loyal service to you will bring some of you round eventually to accepting Marxist policies in general.' He suddenly raised his voice. 'But you will fail to achieve your purposes, just as abysmally as they have always failed to achieve theirs.'

He jumped down from the chair-arm he'd been sitting on.

'You will fail because you've not got the support of the working-class of this country.'

He stood still with his back to the chair, his short legs rigid, his heavy shoulders hunched, his face protruding towards her. A slight flush had appeared on his cheeks, making her realise how waxily pallid his complexion had seemed till now.

'We have a great deal of support from trade-unionists,' she said.

'Not from the rank-and-file, who often don't even support their own shop stewards these days. You won't get the working-class of this country on your side any more than the Marxists will, and the reason you won't is that we, the ruling-class, have long ago bought the workers off, we've bribed them, we've hooked them by offering them a minimal share of the super-profits we extract from the Third World

93

and now they neither think of themselves as working-class nor do they have the least knowledge of socialist ideas. So when we find ourselves in economic trouble as at present, and they become restive because of the cuts we are obliged to make in their standard of living, we have only to crack the whip of unemployment over them and they come to heel.'

'You talk as if you were a Marxist parodying the views of a capitalist,' she said.

He smiled for the first time since she had come upon him in the garden.

'I *am* a Marxist,' he said complacently. 'In the sense that I have taken care to acquaint myself thoroughly with Marxist writings. I believe that in order to defeat our most formidable enemy we must understand him.'

'I agree,' she said.

He either did not detect her irony or he ignored it. He went on, 'The only part of the world where the working-class – as distinct from the peasantry – shows any sign of revolt is in communist-ruled eastern Europe.'

'Then why does your government try to persuade the public that the Red Army, in spite of the likelihood of revolt in its rear, is poised to commit massive aggression at any moment against the whole of western Europe including Britain?'

'We don't merely try to persuade the public of this – we succeed in persuading them,' he said. 'Even some of your CNDers, who say Britain would be committing suicide if it tried to defend itself with nuclear weapons, have unconsciously been led by us into taking for granted that the Russians would be the attackers.'

'But you yourself don't believe this?'

'Of course not. The Russians might decide to invade one of the communist-ruled countries on their borders – Poland for instance – if it showed signs of breaking its alliance with them and siding with us, but they're not insane and they don't suppose they can win the world for communism by military conquest.'

'So you and your government have been telling the public a deliberate lie.'

He showed no resentment at her word. 'I am a politician serving the interests of the upper class I belong to,' he said. 'I am not a devotee of the truth for its own sake. If it's useful to us I'll use it; if not, not. Though I prefer to be able to use truth rather than lies because it is more effective in the long run.'

'What is your motive for telling this particular lie you've admitted to?'

'Well, what do *you* think our motive is?' His emphasis seemed intended not to be sarcastic but to suggest that he seriously wanted her opinion.

'One of your motives could be to boost the profits of the armaments industry, especially at this time of economic crisis for industry in general,' she said. 'Another could be that you hope to divert away from yourselves and on to a foreign power the hostility your home policies will sooner or later rouse among the majority of the British people.'

'You're right,' he readily said. 'But neither of those motives is our main one. You ought to understand that the Soviet Union actually is a deadly menace to us, though only indirectly at present.'

He moved quickly out of his rigid stance near the arm of his chair and came over towards the fireplace to stand in front of the embroidered screen there. He was nearer to her now, and however upright she might try to sit in her armchair he was in a more dominant position than before, looking down on her. He went on:

'The most immediate danger facing the so-called "West" – if I may use this euphemism by which we capitalists guilefully refer to the major capitalist countries of the world including sometimes Japan – comes from the increasing revolt of the ruined peoples of the Third World whom recently we have more thoroughly robbed, with the aid of local despots friendly to us, than we ever could have done when they were under our own imperial rule. If their revolt were to succeed, and we were to be deprived of the huge tribute we extort from them in interest on our loans to their own tyrants, the present crisis of the West would be almost unimaginably worsened and our working-classes would at long last be driven to rise against us – probably with direct help then from the Soviet Union, which in any case is already supplying arms and advisers to Third World revolutionaries.' He was staring down at her all the while he was speaking. 'It is to prevent this worst ultimate disaster of a world victory for communism that I would unhesitatingly press the nuclear button. And now perhaps you'll appreciate why we think it necessary to keep the general public – the "gormless millions" as they were amusingly called by one of our bishops lately – in a state of constant enmity towards the Soviet Union, whether we do it by telling them truths or lies.'

'What I cannot "appreciate" or understand is how you could press the button in the full knowledge that, even if your government bunker were deep enough underground to keep you temporarily safe, your family and friends and millions of innocent men, women and children would be destroyed by the retaliatory strike that would inevitably follow.'

Anger for the first time momentarily showed in his pallid face.

'I could take that as an insult,' he said. 'I don't mean just your implication that I would dare to press the button only because I myself would expect to survive in a specially impenetrable anti-nuclear shelter; I mean your suggestion that I'd be quite indifferent to the fate of my family and of all the rest of the population of this country, not to mention the human race as a whole. I would have thought you were intelligent enough not to share the assumption common to so many of your fellow campaigners that only they want to avoid nuclear war and that we others are monsters devoid of all humane feelings.'

She said, 'It is absolutely untrue that any of my fellow campaigners think like that.'

He ignored this and went on: 'The very last thing I would *want* to do would be to start a nuclear war. But I would certainly rather be dead than live under communism. So would my family, I know.'

'Including your young grandchildren?' She had seen pictures of them with him in the colour supplement of a Sunday newspaper.

'If my grandchildren should grow up to become adults living in a communist-ruled society they would curse me for having failed to start the holocaust that would have destroyed them in childhood.'

'And would the surviving millions of other human beings curse you for that too?'

'Possibly not. Most of them might be incapable of realising there could be a higher and less robot-like life than the one they would find themselves living then.'

He abruptly moved from in front of the embroidered screen and paced towards his armchair and back again from there towards hers. He said: 'My great fear is that we may not press the button in time. The mobilisation of public feeling by groups like yours, and the action of the peoples of the world, could prevent it. And defeat would creep gradually upon us.'

The tenseness in the posture of his body as he spoke suggested that his 'great fear' was not just a rhetorical expression – it was something he genuinely felt at this moment. But the Victorian screen behind him, embroidered with brightly coloured parrots and parakeets perched on interlacing leafy braches, gave him a deceptive appearance of unreality for an instant, as if he was an actor playing at having got lost in a tropical forest or jungle. He suddenly became real again, saying: 'Of course everything I have said to you today is off the record and strictly between ourselves and you will report none of it in your magazine.'

'I couldn't give you an undertaking not to report any of it.'

There was a heavy silence. Then he said, slowly, 'I don't think you will report any of it.'

She sensed a weight of menace behind his words. He paused for quite a while, as though to make sure she had sensed this, before he went on in a smoother tone.

'If you were able to publish a report I should absolutely deny the truth of it. Our conversation would anyway seem so improbable to most of your readers that they would easily be convinced it was a fiction. You are a short-story writer, aren't you?'

'Well, yes, I am.'

'They would think it was an imaginative spoof – and not a very amusing one.'

Now she was certain that he must have had enquiries made about her. He couldn't otherwise have known she wrote short stories, as she hadn't succeeded in getting any of them published yet.

'Or perhaps you might have the idea of reproducing our conversation as part of a short story and in the pretence that it was all an invention of yours. Let me remind you that besides our law of libel we still have an Official Secrets Act in this country. And you'd better not hope you could shield yourself by disguising the persons and the place you were writing about, because unless the disguise was so thorough that no one could possibly guess the real origin of your story you would still run the risk that *someone*,' he paused significantly, 'might claim to recognise persons or place or both.'

He turned from her to go towards a large table in the middle of the room. As he went he added sardonically, 'And in any case, even supposing you weren't found guilty of libel or of contravening the Official Secrets Act, you would still be giving birth to a mongrel which would have no integrity either as political reportage or as a work of art.'

He moved round the table to an upright chair on the other side of it. He sat down and reached across the table to pull towards himself a wire tray containing papers, one of which he lifted out to look at. He was pointedly ignoring her, and seemed set to continue doing so. The door of the room opened. The tall wardress-like woman came in, without having knocked. She had a look of expectancy, as though she had been summoned by him. Perhaps he had pressed with his foot on a bell-push concealed beneath the carpet.

'Oh,' he said, raising his eyes at last, 'Irma, would you please show Ms Faulder out – by the front way.'

Miriam was aware that he said 'miz' not with any anti-feminist sneer in his tone but as if 'miz' was no less acceptable to him than the traditional 'missiz' or 'miss'. However, he did not say goodbye to her. Nor did she to him.

She followed Irma out of the room, and Irma preceded her also along the passage outside, walking very upright with strides which gave the impression of being shorter than they would naturally have been if she had worn a less narrow skirt. Miriam, staring at Irma's back, all at once re-membered the minister's words 'I don't think you will report any of it.' Irma did not look round at her. They were approaching a side passage on their right. Where was Frooms? They passed the passage. He did not come out of it, and they arrived at the front door. Irma stopped by the door, standing movelessly there, making clear that she expected Miriam to let herself out. The iron doorhandle was so stiff that Miriam had to use both hands to turn it. How easily at that moment Irma and Frooms could have seized hold of her from behind. She was quite glad to get out on to the short driveway and hurry along it to reach the wrought-iron gates. They opened almost easily.

She was halfway along the stretch of road leading towards the lych gate outside which her car was, when an ominous fancy came into her mind. Suppose that a high-ranking and ruthlessly ambitious politician knew that some ordinary woman or man had information about him which could ruin him politically if it became public, mightn't he arrange to have this ordinary person eliminated in such a way that it might appear to be the work of terrorists intending to assassinate the politician himself? For instance, if the person had left a car somewhere near the politician's house while going to visit him, mightn't the police assume that a bomb exploding underneath the car when it was driven away again had been placed beneath it by someone who had mistaken it for the politician's own? No; political conditions in Britain had not reached such a stage where it would be a common thing for prominent politicians to commit small-scale privately-motivated murders. Not yet, she thought. Nevertheless, when she reached her car again outside the lych gate she bent down to look at the road underneath the engine, though only for a moment because she didn't want any local villager to see her looking and perhaps to come forward with an offer of help on the assumption that the car had developed a mechanical fault. She noticed nothing abnormal under the engine. She got into the car and drove quickly off. There was no explosion.

She felt a relief, which she was immediately ashamed of, not just because her suspicion that there might be a bomb attached to the car seemed a little paranoid to her now, but more still because she knew she had no right to regard her own destruction as having any importance compared with the vast annihilation of life that this minister – and there must be many like him – was prepared to bring about all over the earth. Yet as she drove on down a springtime lane, taking an indirect route home to avoid passing the manor-house again, she recognised that she felt more optimistic than she had before coming to see him. His 'great fear' that the massive use of nuclear weapons might be delayed until popular opinion and worldwide resistance made it impossible had given her a new and stronger hope.

The White-Pinafored Black Cat

IT MIGHT have been better if Esther Johnson and her brother Maurice had retired to a proper village with a church and a pub and four or five little shops, rather than to this hamlet without any of those advantages. What had attracted Maurice was the railway station here, a small one out of use as a station after the single line passing through it had been closed down early on in the post-Second World War period of railway dismantlements; and Maurice – a railway enthusiast since childhood – had discovered during a summer holiday with Esther in this district that the station house was up for sale to the public. The price asked for it was almost unbelievably low, and he decided at once to buy it. Esther acquiesced; though while she quite liked the prospect of retiring to an address that would intrigue her few surviving old friends, she could have wished it had been one that would have sounded a little more fashionable perhaps, such as 'The Old Watermill' or even 'The Old Coach House'.

But the station house was comfortable to live in, more so than a converted watermill or coach house would probably have been. It was well-built and pleasant to look at and on its south side it had a garden already plentifully provided with flowering plants, and also there was a lawn that sloped slightly downwards to a clear-flowing stream. Maurice would have liked to retain in the house the old ticket office together with the short passage-way which led out from this to the station platform on the north side; however, Esther was firmly against that idea, although when telling him so she tempered her firmness with a pun. 'I must absolutely draw the line at our pretending to be station-master and station-mistress here,' she said. She knew that few things would have pleased him better now than to be in charge of a rural railway station where real trains actually stopped and he could sell and collect tickets; and certainly she would have been glad sometimes if she could have made the short direct train journey to the nearest shopping centre instead of having to take the considerably longer road route there by bus or on her bicycle, much though she still enjoyed cycling. Fortunately, after they had found an efficient local builder who was able to convert the ticket office and its adjoining passage-way into one room where Maurice could set up a model railway track, he acknowledged that the conversion was an improvement.

Retirement was never a problem for him. Every morning he woke to an awareness of something interesting he would be able to do, either in his model railway room or outside at the end of the platform in the old signal box which became his workshop where he could make useful or ornamental things for the house or for his railway, and later on he took up pen-and-ink sketching, mainly of scenes that would have been viewable formerly by train travellers along the now rail-less track. It was just as well he could be so self-sufficient, Esther thought, as he was not a man who easily found new friends. He was inclined to be jokily outspoken in a way which seemed to her to be obviously not at all ill-natured, but it gave lasting offence sometimes to people who had not known him long. One of these was Dr Vallance their nearest doctor here, to whom Maurice had unluckily remarked when consulting him about an attack of indigestion, 'Of course you doctors nowadays are really Civil Servants', and after that Dr Vallance had refused to have him as a patient any more. Maurice, unworried, said to Esther, 'He never did my indigestion the slightest good. From now on I shall avoid all doctors for as long as I possibly can.' But Esther felt she needed to see one because of her arthritis – if that's what it was – which was beginning to affect her shoulders as well as the finger joints of her left hand, and being too embarrassed to return to Dr Vallance (though presumably he wouldn't have refused to continue accepting her as a patient) she had to go to Dr Pentelow whose surgery was a mile farther away than Dr Vallance's.

Maurice's jocular frankness didn't get him liked by any of the inhabitants of the hamlet. Not that any of them showed hostility to him, and to Esther they were always civil, though she sensed that – no doubt because of Maurice – their civility was unlikely ever to develop into friendliness. She did not mind greatly. She found friendliness – and one particular friend, Margery Horton – among the small congregation at the church of a nearby village, a beautiful seventeenth-century church not attended by any of the few other Anglicans living in the hamlet, who regarded Mr Liddicott, the rector, as standoffish, and preferred to go to a church in the nearest town or to listen to the Sunday service on the radio. It was Margery who gave Esther and Maurice the kitten they named Abigail which had such attractive markings – all black except for one large pure white oblong patch stretching downwards from just below the chin, like a pinafore. They were glad to have Abigail as a companion for Selima, their older cat which they had brought with them from their former home in London when they had retired. Selima was already ten years old now, and Esther had recognised that without a cat at all she, if not Maurice, might begin to feel increasingly isolated here in this hamlet as she too grew older. And she became more and more fond of Abigail, who seemed to show an attachment to her personally in a way that even Selima, affectionate but caring less for persons than for places, never did. Nearly always as she returned from the town on those mornings when she went shopping there she would find Abigail sitting upright just inside the garden gate, waiting for her, and she would say 'You faithful little creature'; at which Abigail would turn and precede her along the path to the station house. But one morning when she returned from taking Selima – who had been refusing food recently – to see the vet, she did not find Abigail waiting for her. Esther was tired as she walked into the kitchen carrying the wicker basket in which she had taken Selima on the bus to the town and back. She wished Maurice had been able to come with her to carry Selima, as he gladly would have done if he hadn't been feeling unwell after breakfast. Abigail was not in the kitchen when Esther opened the lid of the basket to release Selima there. Esther found Abigail dozing in the south room on the hearth rug at the sprawled and upturned feet of Maurice who was sitting dead in his armchair. The pain he had had after breakfast had been due to heart disease, not indigestion.

The shock for Esther was very great, although its full effect was held back by the pressure of all the things she had to do now, immediately and during the following week, and without any help from the one person she would most naturally have turned to in a time of disaster, Maurice himself. She did get support, however, from her friend Margery, especially when arrangements had to be made with the undertaker and the rector for the funeral. In spite of arthritis which was more severe than Esther's yet was, Margery came over to the hamlet each day before the funeral and stayed at the station house for several days and nights after it to help with the shopping and cooking and to keep Esther company in the evening. But eventually Esther was alone there, except for the two cats, and her grief came fully into its own.

Perhaps only the cats, and the necessity of feeding them, made her take the trouble to go on preparing meals for herself also, though her thoughts and feelings were about Maurice and hardly at all about the cooking or eating or anything else she had to continue doing now. To have been able to talk about him with someone who had known him really well might have given her comfort, but none of their surviving old friends had been in good enough health to come down for the funeral, and their father and mother were dead and so were all their other relatives except for their cousins who lived in Australia. Yet she could get some comfort from talking about him in her thoughts, and the presence of Selima and Abigail in the room helped her to feel as if she wasn't talking entirely to herself. On the first evening that she was alone with them she did once speak directly to them about him, though not aloud. 'He used to stand at the back door and call you in by name every evening before it got dark,' she said to them in her thoughts. How anxious he would become if they did not return quickly, she remembered. His voice would rise till the whole hamlet must have heard it and perhaps laughed not very kindly about him and about those unusual names Selima and Abigail. He was afraid that the two cats might take to hunting together down by the river in the long grass where adders lurked. Or that they would 'go feral' and never come home to the house again. 'Feral' had been a favourite word of his ever since he had first read it in a boys' magazine during his schooldays. He had never really outgrown his boyhood. He had not wanted to outgrow it, or to adapt himself fully to adult life. She had long realised, though never so keenly as she did now on her first evening alone in the room with Selima and Abigail, that this was a fault in him. He might still be alive and have several more years of life before him if his boyishly tactless jokiness hadn't offended Dr Vallance. Yet she had not at any time in the past wished to reproach him for his boyishness, and least of all did she wish to now that he was gone. How much more forgivable a fault his was, she thought, than the forgetfulness that some adults showed about their early years.

For many evenings in her aloneness with Selima and Abigail she told them, not aloud, the story of his and her childhood at the vicarage. She was two and a half years younger than Maurice, yet except during her earliest infancy he had shared his toys with her, so that soon she became as interested in his trains as he already was in her dolls. He was imaginative, not only about the dolls and the trains, and he shared his imaginings with her. There was one of his imaginings which meant so much to her now that she repeated the story of it on several evenings in her thoughts. It had come to him the day when he and she had discovered in the box-room at the top of the house an oblong tin which had once contained shortbread. The tin was brilliantly rustless inside, with only small spots of rust showing here and there through the tartan-patterned paper that covered the outside. He carried it downstairs, concealing it under his jersey and trying to conceal with his arm the bulge it made, and she knew it was to be a secret from everyone else in the house – their governess, their mother and father, even the cook and the housemaid. They took it on to the veranda, and from a corner behind the wicker armchair there he fetched out a strange-shaped white stone they had hidden after bringing it back from the seaside that summer. He put the stone into the tin and closed the lid over it. 'This must never be opened again,' he said. 'Now let's take it to the park.' They set out at once for the public park, which was less than a quarter of a mile away, and when they got there they walked to the far end of it where the disused sand-pit was. He pushed the tin into one of the larger of the many holes excavated in the face of the pit by nesting sand-martins. She helped to enlarge the hole, after they had made sure there was no nest inside it, and then to fill it up with sand around the tin. She didn't know why they were doing this, nor did she ask him. They stepped back when the tin was completely and deeply hidden by firmly pressed sand. They stood silent till Maurice said, 'This is the most important thing in the world. It is more important even than Mummy and Daddy.' She felt an excitement, yet she was a little frightened – not only because she suspected that their vicar father would have thought there was something heathen about what they were doing, and that their mother – although she was less strict in her beliefs and was fond of theatricals – would have been rather shocked. Esther was frightened also at the idea that anything in the world, except God, could be more important to her than her mother and father. And Maurice was saying that an old shortbread tin was more important. But she sensed that it wasn't just the tin itself he was thinking of. And then, not quite clearly at first yet clearly enough to cause her excitement to overcome her fear, she knew he was really saying that he and she, through their act of burying the tin in the sandpit, had become more important to each other than either their mother or their father was to them. After that, if not because of it, they became consciously closer to each other in affection and in understanding as they grew older, until the time came for Maurice to go away to his public school, while she, being a girl, went to the local High School. (Her mother would have liked her to go to Cheltenham Ladies' College if it had been less expensive and if her father hadn't believed that young girls should live at home.) But

Maurice wrote to her often from his boarding school. She kept most of his letters. She still had them, though it was years since she'd last read any of them. She had brought them with her when she and Maurice had moved from London to the station house. They were in a cardboard box at the back of her wardrobe upstairs.

She fetched them down to the sitting-room and began to read them in the evenings now, slowly and not aloud, each of them more than once. It had been usual for Abigail to jump on to her lap and lie there to be stroked while Esther talked about Maurice in her thoughts, but stroking Abigail while at the same time handling the letters wasn't easy for Esther, who was thankful that Abigail was such a good cat and didn't ever try to paw or claw at the letters out of curiosity, or out of jealousy because they were monopolising Esther's attention. Selima did not jump on to Esther's lap. Poor Selima was no longer able to do that. She had slowly been getting weaker, and the vet hadn't held out much hope that she could ever fully recover. So it was an additional sadness more than an unexpected shock for Esther to find her lying dead on the hearth rug one morning. Esther would have liked to make a grave for Selima at the bottom of the garden, but though still capable of pulling up weeds by hand and of planting small plants with a trowel, she could not dig with a spade any more. She had to get the vet to come and take Selima away.

After this she was even more thankful for the comforting that Maurice's letters from school gave her as she continued reading them in the evenings with Abigail on her lap. There was one of them in which he was enthusiastic about Thomas Gray's poem 'On a Favourite Cat, Drowned in a Tub of Gold Fishes'. It was a kind of poem he liked better than Gray's more serious 'Elegy written in a Country Church-yard' and he wanted her to like it too – which she did, – and nearly fifty years later their own Selima had been so named by them because as a kitten she had had a fondness for looking into bowls and vases of all sorts, though fortunately never meeting the same fate as Gray's Selima. At the age of fifteen Maurice began writing light verse himself, some of which he enclosed in his letters, and by the time he reached the Sixth Form several of his poems had already appeared in the school magazine. He was expected by everyone to do well academically. Their father hoped he would go to Oxford and from there into the Administrative Civil Service. But victory in the Great War was longer coming than their father had prayed it would be, and Maurice was called up into the army at the end of 1917. Esther could find no letters of his written to her after this. She couldn't even remember for certain that he had written any to her then, though it seemed likely to her now that he would have done. The whole of that year, from his call-up until the Armistice, had become vague to her, possibly because she had given so little thought to it – she hadn't wanted to think of it – during later years. One evening while she was trying to make herself remember Maurice as he had been when he had come home from the war she fell asleep in her chair, and when she woke – or just before she was fully awake – she felt an intense physical pain, the most dreadful pain she had yet had in all her life, a pain that could mean she was on the point of death.

She could not locate just where in her body it was centred. At first it seemed to be in her chest and then in her throat and then it spread to her shoulders and her arms. It was a general, paralysing pain. But its intensity lessened as it spread, and when she became quite wide awake she couldn't feel it anywhere. Yet for many minutes she remained convinced it had been a physical reality, not just a horrible dream. She got up out of her chair, only then becoming remorsefully aware that Abigail, who was forced to jump to the floor, had been lying on her lap unstroked and unthought of by her all this while. But soon, remembering why she had got up, she temporarily forgot Abigail again. She had intended to go and telephone Dr Pentelow. She wished now more than ever before that the dislike Maurice had developed for the telephone during his years of office work in London hadn't made him refuse to have one installed in the house here. 'There's a call-box just across the road anyway', he had said, not considering the possibility that he or she might become physically incapable of getting across to it one day or even merely that the weather might sometimes be bad. She thought she could hear rain falling now. Yes, it was, heavily. And what would Dr Pentelow's response be when she did go across to the call-box and phone him? Would she be able to persuade him that she was ill enough to make it absolutely necessary for him after his day's work to get into his car and drive over at once to see her? No, she wouldn't be able to, because she was becoming less and less sure that the pain hadn't been a mere nightmare after all. She decided to postpone ringing up Dr Pentelow till the morning. She went back to her chair, at the foot of which Abigail sat waiting, giving no sign of grievance at having been tipped abruptly by Esther to the floor. To make amends for that unkindness Esther bent down and stroked Abigail fondly now, but did not get into the chair again. A feeling of shakiness caused her to think that the best thing to do would be to go upstairs and, early though it was, to put herself to bed for the night.

She went to see Dr Pentelow after her breakfast next morning. She felt no unusual pain now, only the usual arthritic one across her shoulders and also the one that had started fairly recently in her legs and was particularly noticeable this morning as she walked the five hundred yards or so between the bus stop and Dr Pentelow's house. She would certainly tell him about this as well as about her

114

experience the previous evening. He took her blood-pressure, then applied his stethoscope to various places on her chest and her back, but he made no comment until she asked whether what she'd experienced could have been a kind of hallucination caused perhaps partly by the anti-arthritic drugs she had been taking. He said this was unlikely; however he prescribed a new drug, which he hoped would help her legs too. She must let him know how she got on with it. He said goodbye to her very pleasantly. And by the time she returned home again, having first taken the bus into the town to have the prescription made up by the chemist, she was almost wholly convinced that her nightmare had been of no, or very little, medical importance.

She didn't suspect there was any connection between it and her sudden ability, as she sat with Abigail on her lap the following evening, to begin to remember things about Maurice during the final year of the Great War. The first thing she clearly remembered was his being at home in the vicarage drawing-room wearing his army uniform. Their mother and father and several friends were there and so was Mavis Prosser , whom he'd become engaged to just before he was sent to France. Mavis was looking up at his face in an adoringly admiring way, which was perfectly genuine, and was asking him to tell them about some of the things he had done in battle. He flushed, and wouldn't say anything. The others probably thought this was due to modesty, but Esther could detect an extreme distaste in his look. After he was demobbed he broke off his engagement with Mavis. He never got married. It was as if the war had turned him against all the ways of the adult world. He even stopped going to church, in spite of the distress this gave their father and mother. He refused to take any job which would have put him in a position of authority over other people. He didn't become soured, or a rebel; he simply seemed to regard the adult world as a joke, a rather stupid joke. He once told her that the epitaph he would like to have inscribed on his tomb-stone was John Gay's: 'Life is a jest, and all things show it; I thought so once, but now I know it.' He never lost his liking for verse, nor his other boyhood interests. Nor his affection for her. Had some particular happening during the war been the cause of the lifelong change in him afterwards? Or would he have developed just as he did if there had been no war? She couldn't believe he would have. Perhaps the death of his friend Louis was the cause. As Esther said this in her thoughts she had a premonitory feeling that the night-mare pain she had experienced two evenings ago was about to come upon her again, though this time she was wide awake.

She quickly lifted Abigail down from her lap to the safety on the floor, and at the moment she did so she understood that the pain which was threatening to return had been connected with Louis. But there was a difference now: she was aware of the connection, as she hadn't been two evenings ago, and a hope came to her that she might be able to use her awareness to fend off the pain, or at least to change it, to convert it from a physical pain which she could not deal with to one in the mind which she possibly could. She began to tell herself the story of Louis. He was Maurice's best friend at school, and Maurice had invited him to stay at the vicarage for a day or two during several of the school holidays. He was a musician, a very promising pianist. She was learning to play the piano then. She used to turn over the pages of the music for him as he played Mozart sonatas on her mother's baby-grand Blüthner in the drawing-room. The day he came to say goodbye to them before he was sent to France she was alone with him in the drawing-room for a minute or two. They were standing near the piano, facing each other. The words rose into her mind, 'You are in love with me, Louis.' She came very near to speaking them to him. She had no doubt they were true, and she knew she was in love with him. But he did not say anything either. He may have thought that at the age of fifteen and a half she was too young to become engaged to him, and that he would wait for another half year before asking her father's permission to marry her. He was killed four days after he was sent to the Front. She never in later years became engaged to anyone, although there were two men at different times who wanted to marry her. She could not be in love with either of them, and she was not the sort of woman who believes that almost any husband is better than none. But she had wanted to be married, and now she was old and getting older and more arthritic and Margery her friend was seldom able to come to see her, and the rector, Mr Liddicott, never did.

'That's quite enough of that,' she told herself, and immediately afterwards she realised she had said it aloud; so she stroked Abigail, who might have recognised reproof in the tone of it, and she added aloud, 'I was speaking to myself, not to you, Abigail dear.' Then she went on, not aloud, to tell herself she ought to be thankful that things weren't worse than they were with her, that she was still able to go to church, to do her own shopping, to visit Margery, to weed and to plant in the garden with her knee-pads on, that there was a boy from the hamlet who mowed the lawn for her, that even the adults in the hamlet had seemed friendlier to her since Maurice had died. And although she had never married she had been able for nearly twenty-five years of her life to do work which she loved as a teacher of young children at a preparatory school. Her father had expected her as an unmarried daughter to stay at home with her parents, but in fact it was their bachelor son Maurice who found an office job near enough to the vicarage for him to continue living with them, and when Mother had to leave the vicarage after

Father died Maurice moved with her to another house in London not far from the office. Esther was very successful in her teaching of eight- and nine-year-old children, as everyone recognised, not least Commander Eversley, the chairman of the governing body which her headmaster, Mr Winford, had got together so that his school should acquire charitable status (and the tax advantages this brought with it). Nevertheless when Mother died and Maurice promptly gave up his job as an insurance broker's clerk and said he wanted to get out of London, Esther agreed to retire from teaching and to set up house with him in the country somewhere. Her last end-of-term at the school was a sad one, made sadder by Commander Eversley's goodbye talk alone with her. 'You won't need a pension from the school, of course,' he said, after praising her work. No doubt he had been told by Mr Winford that her mother had left her enough to live on, but she knew that two of the men teachers who had retired since the governing body had come into existence, and neither of whom was without private means, were receiving small pensions from the school. She had burst into tears in front of the Commander, and she still – to this day, to this evening – felt ashamed of that. But she had felt no bitterness at the time about her treatment by the governors, and she must not let herself feel any now – nor about Mr Liddicott's failure to come and visit her at the station-house, though she couldn't help comparing him unfavourably with her father, who would never have neglected one of his elderly and solitary parishioners in this way. She must count her blessings, and Abigail was not the least of these. She must put the remainder of her life to good use, try each day to do the things she knew she ought to do. And one of these things – as she had been increasingly aware recently – was to see her solicitor about certain changes that needed to be made in her will. After all, even if her nightmare pain had not been due to any fatal physical malady, she was not going to live for ever.

On a Friday morning – Friday being a usual shopping day for her – she visited the solicitor; and that evening with Abigail on her lap again she began to speak, at first only in her thoughts, about the two codicils she had asked the solicitor to add to her will. She would rather not have spoken about them at all; because one of them was painful for her to think of, but as it concerned Abigail who was lying warm on her lap she would have felt like a deceiver if she had kept it out of her talk now. She nevertheless delayingly spoke to begin with about the other codicil, which bequeathed most of her estate to the fund for repairing the seventeenth-century church that she loved and continued worshipping at each Sunday morning in spite of the rector's neglect of her. At last she said out loud, 'Abigail dear, oh Abigail, there is something I need to tell you though I know you are not able to understand me. If only you could understand, I could discuss it with you and get your agreement to what I have done. Or perhaps you would disagree. Then I would respect your disagreement, and I would make the solicitor cancel the codicil about you that I told him to add to my will when I saw him this morning. But as I have not become senile enough yet to think that you and I can really talk to each other, Abigail dear, I know I must rely on my own judgement, and it tells me that if I died tomorrow there would be no one to care for you and to feed you. I would have asked Margery, who gave you to me when you were a kitten, to take you back if I were to die before her, but I grieve to say that her arthritis is becoming so bad that soon she may no longer be able to care even for herself. So I felt I had no alternative to doing what I did this morning. Oh Abigail, I have added a request to my will that as soon as I am dead the vet should come here and put you to sleep. Oh Abigail, forgive me, forgive me, and believe that I have done what

I'm sure will be best for you, though if you could understand what I'm saying you might tell me you would rather risk trying to survive without me.'

She stopped speaking aloud. She recognised that if she went on like this she might before long get herself into a state of believing that Abigail could after all understand everything she said. And it might be better for her to stop talking to Abigail even in her thoughts. It might be better if she stopped talking in her thoughts altogether and found an evening occupation more likely to do no harm to her health of mind. There had never been television in the house for her to watch, because Maurice wouldn't have been able to bear it, and the wireless which he could just tolerate made him restless and she used it so seldom that when it got out of order a year ago she hadn't bothered to have it repaired. They relied on *The Times* and the local paper for their news. She still took both of these, but she couldn't occupy whole evenings reading them. She decided she would have the wireless repaired. Also she would start reading her favourite author, Jane Austen, again.

Next morning, though it was a Saturday and the town would be crowded with shoppers, she took the bus and went to ask the man at the small electricity shop if he would collect and repair her wireless set, which she told him was an old one too heavy for her to carry. He said he would come on Monday. She went straight back to the bus stop, having no shopping to do as she had done it all on Friday. When she got back to the hamlet she was a little disappointed not to find Abigail waiting for her at the gate of the station house garden. Abigail was nowhere in the garden and remained away from the house all day. Before dark Esther went to the back door just as Maurice used to do when the two cats were late in returning for their evening milk, and she called out the name of Abigail, her voice rising as his used to rise if the cats did not return quickly to his call, though her call was shriller than his; yet Abigail did not come. She was about to give up, when suddenly a cat peered in through the garden gate. Although she soon knew it wasn't Abigail it caused her to remain here and to continue calling for a while, but without effect. Abigail did not come back that night and Esther did not sleep.

She was up early in the morning, well before the milkman had begun his round. There was still no sign of Abigail. When the milkman came to the door she asked him if he had seen anything of her cat, which she described to him. He told her he would recognise Abigail anywhere. He was a kind-faced, youngish man with a dark beard and a high bald forehead. 'I'm afraid I've not seen her this morning,' he said. 'But I'll keep a good look-out in future.' After he had gone Esther wrote out in large letters on a piece of white card a notice headed with the word MISSING and mentioning Abigail's unusual markings and friendly nature. She wrapped the notice in a transparent plastic bag, as a protection against bad weather, and she pinned it with drawing pins to the outside of the garden gate where everyone walking by would see it. Several of the neighbours spoke to her about it during the next few days, though only to ask whether she had had any news yet of where Abigail might have got to. The days and the nights passed, and Abigail did not return.

One morning the moment came when she gave up hope of ever seeing Abigail again. She was at the back door, paying the milkman what she owed him for the week's milk. He told her that on his rounds he had asked at every house whether anyone had caught sight of her cat anywhere, and no one had. There was real sympathy in his voice. She had difficulty in holding back her tears. Her sadness was made worse by a sudden thought that Abigail while not understanding her

121

words about the codicil in her will might somehow have sensed danger in them and might instinctively have chosen to 'go feral' rather than remain with her. Only by immediately reminding herself of another favourite saying of Maurice's, 'Few things are more frequent than coincidences', was she able to become sure that Abigail's disappearance had not been an instinctive act of self-preservation but a dreadful coincidence. Yet her sureness could not prevent her from having an intense brief feeling that there was nothing ahead for her now except ageing and aloneness and illness and death. The kind and helpful milkman, just before going off to his next customer, said to her, 'I won't give up keeping a look-out for Abigail.' Words came into her mind which she might almost have spoken to him if he had stayed a little longer at her door. As she carried into the kitchen the bottle of milk he had left for her she spoke them aloud to herself, 'If I didn't believe that my heavenly father is watching over me I don't know what I would do.'

At the Ferry Inn

ARNOLD OLNEY after forty years of estrangement from his once close friend Walter Selwyn had a letter by the first post one morning in Walter's characteristically almost illegible handwriting to say he would be arriving on the ferry-boat at 11.45 am and was hoping very much to have some hours with Arnold before returning to London for his flight back to New York the next day. Arnold was only momentarily disconcerted at the risk Walter had taken in giving him such short notice – so short that if the letter had come by the second post Arnold would not have seen it till the evening, because he had planned to be out all day, and what might be the one opportunity he would ever have of meeting Walter again would have been lost. When he got into his car to drive to the ferry he felt an extreme gladness, and he realised at last how profoundly during the past few years he had wished to be reconciled with Walter, though he ought long before now to have guessed this if merely from the frequency of his dreams at night about Walter as the young poet he used to know so well and to admire more than any other.

The ferry-boat was coming out from the mouth of the estuary on the other side of the water as Arnold walked to the quay after leaving his car in the nearby car park. The boat moved against a background of high-masted small moored yachts and of trees dark enough to be firs or cypresses though their rounded cumulus-cloudlike shapes told him they were neither firs nor cypresses but possibly oaks or not yet diseased elms. Above them the sky was heavy with grey horizontal clouds. The boat turned gradually from the shadowed mainland until its bow was pointing directly towards him, so that he could no longer see its side or know whether its movement was slow or fast, and after a while he felt that his staring at its bow was making it seem to have stopped moving. He looked away from it, to the right and to the left, at the intermittently sunlit grey water, sparkling in patches here and there yet elsewhere as unrippled as though it had been smoothed over with a flat iron, and he saw a cormorant coming from a distance on his left in rapid straight flight parallel to the near shoreline and so low that its wing tips almost contacted their dark reflections on the water's surface. He watched it pass and go blackly on out of sight. He was taken by surprise when he noticed that the ferry-boat was already nearly half-way across from the mainland towards the quay where he was waiting. He could see the passengers on the deck, even their faces, though none of these distinctly yet. A quick fear rose in him. Walter might have changed so much as to be unrecognisable by him, might appear not just old but senile and decrepit. The thought of this was hardly bearable to him. When the ferry-boat came nearer he could see no one on it who looked at all as he could have expected Walter to look, and he had a different fear: that Walter since writing to him might have had second thoughts and decided against making the journey to meet him. Even after the ferry-boat was alongside the quay and the passengers were beginning to walk down the gangway, Arnold could not see Walter among them. Then a young man still on the deck waved to him. Arnold was totally unable to believe for a second or two that this could be Walter. But as the young man descended on to the quay he did not seem so young. Rather than really young he was astoundingly well-preserved. He certainly was Walter – tall, broad-hipped, sloping-shouldered, his hatless hair thick and yellow, his cheeks plump and smooth-skinned as ever. He was wearing an alkanet-blue light summer jacket and was not carrying a raincoat or a bag of any kind or a book. His face as he came up to Arnold showed the kind of pleasure it would have shown more than forty years ago if they had met again after not having seen each other for a week or two.

'How glad I am you're here,' he said. 'I was afraid you might not get my letter in time.'

'How glad I am I did get it,' Arnold said.

'I ought to have written sooner, but I didn't start reading your new book till the day before yesterday. I think it's wonderful.'

In an instant the anti-progressive attitudes and ideas which had been adopted by Walter during the past forty years, and had inhibited Arnold from trying to renew his friendship with Walter, became entirely unimportant to Arnold, and he said,

'There's no one I would rather hear praise my book than you.'

'It made me realise how much I needed to meet you again,' Walter said. 'I only wish I didn't have to go back to London so soon today.'

Though already knowing from Walter's letter that Walter wouldn't be staying for long, Arnold felt a brief chill of disappointment which he attempted to hide by saying in a lively way,

'Well, I hope there'll be time for us to have lunch together at the Ferry Inn just up the road here, and to have a drink beforehand.'

'Oh yes. Plenty of time.'

They began to walk along the cobbled road towards the inn. Arnold said,

'How extraordinary it is that you are actually here. It reminds me of that sonnet of Auden's which begins, "Just as his dream foretold, he met them all." I dreamt two nights ago that I met you here at the ferry.'

'And who were the others – "them all" – you met besides me?' Walter asked, with a keenness which suggested he hadn't yet lost the liking he'd had as a young man for analysing his friend's dreams.

'There weren't any others. Immediately after meeting you I woke.' Arnold, remembering there had been things in his dream that he didn't want to be led into describing to Walter – such as the shock he had got on seeing how saggingly old the flesh of Walter's face had become – hoped to deflect Walter's curiosity by adding,

'How well Auden's sonnet gets the inconsequent feeling of a dream, though not so marvellously as you get it in your poem about the Timor Sea, which is really a poem about Fear.'

'I was always glad you liked that,' Walter said, with such warmth that Arnold wondered whether in spite of Walter's having become world-known (or known at least to those minorities in the world who took notice of modern poets) he had felt a lack among his readers of the kind of whole-hearted enthusiasm shown for his poetry by Arnold in the nineteen thirties. But Arnold wasn't able to say anything further now in praise of the Timor Sea poem, because Walter asked quite eagerly,

'And what happened in your dream *before* you met me?'

They had already reached the front of the Ferry Inn, a genuinely old timber-framed building with a not very wide entrance doorway, and as they were about to go in through this Arnold said,

'A man wearing a green velour homburg hat handed me a suitcase in the street and said, "I'm afraid I've got to hurry so please put this down for me on the steps of the Imperial Bank over there", then left me holding the case which I at once went to get rid of outside the bank before walking very quickly away to meet you at the ferry.'

The passage-way they entered was lined with black oak panels and was narrow, dark and long. As they emerged into the bar-room at the end of it, which by contrast seemed light and was moderately noisy with talk, Walter said,

'So you deposited a bomb in front of the bank.'

The talk immediately stopped, at least from the group of navy-blue-blazered yachtsmen – or so Arnold took them to be – who were standing near the bar that Walter and Arnold were approaching. Walter had spoken in a clear unlowered voice, just as he usually would have done years ago when saying things to his friends which could outrage or alarm other people overhearing him, and he seemed just as indifferent now as he would have been then to the effect he had had on his overhearers. He gave no sign of noticing the looks on the faces of the yachtsmen as he stood waiting at the bar to be served – after insisting that he and not Arnold should be the one to buy the drinks, a schooner of dry sherry for Arnold and a large gin and vermouth for himself.

'A schooner of sherry,' he said to Arnold with interest; 'is that British yachting slang, do you think?'

'I don't know,' Arnold said, without giving even a half-glance towards the four large-bodied blazered men he was standing so close to. He wondered whether the hostility he sensed in them could be defused if he were to say now to Walter, 'I only dreamed I deposited the bomb', but something, he didn't know what, warned him that this might heighten rather than lessen their suspicions. He felt relief when he and Walter began walking away from the bar with the drinks which the impassive barmaid soon brought, though he was as sure as if he could still see the men that all four were staring hard at the backs of the two of them.

He led the way to a small table in an alcove at the far end of the bar-room where no one else was sitting. It was rather dark here both because of the oak panelling and because there were none of the windows with leaded diamond-shaped panes that made the rest of the room a little lighter than the long passage through which he and Walter had entered.

'It's like being born again in reverse,' Walter said after they had sat down. 'First the vaginal passage-way and now the primal snuggery.'

This time the yachtsmen did not appear to hear him, though he spoke no more quietly than before. All four of the men were facing the bar now. The broadness of each of their backs was made to seem still broader as they stood side by side together.

'A strange kind of womb,' Arnold said.

The alcove where he and Walter were sitting was walled on three sides by oak panelling with framed small colour prints of yachting and fox-hunting scenes attached to it, and all along the top of it was a ledge on which brilliantly polished brass horse-harness ornaments were arranged in a continuous row.

But Walter, who had never been as interested as Arnold was in external details, gave only a brief glance round the harness brasses and colour prints, then came back to what evidently interested him much more, Arnold's dream.

'That bomb you let yourself be tricked into leaving outside the bank,' he said with a hint of severity, though smiling, 'obviously represents a residual guilt in you after your years of left-wing political activity.'

Arnold, while unwilling to accept this interpretation, did

not want to interrupt Walter, who went on,

'You were loyal for longer than the rest of us to "the clever hopes", as Auden afterwards called them, that we all fell for in the nineteen thirties, but your book has brilliantly rejected them at last, and without any exhibitionistic breast-beating or spitting on your youth.'

Arnold's unease at Walter's assumption that he had wholly changed his political views since the 'thirties was soothed by a recognition of the strength and genuineness of Walter's admiration for his book.

'I ought certainly to have become deconverted much sooner from my total faith in Stalin,' Arnold said. 'My doubts began quite early on, but I overcame each of them in turn, though less and less easily, until after he died and Khrushchev's revelations about him brought them to their climax. Then quantity changed into quality.' Arnold smiled as he used this dialectical expression, but he saw Walter wince slightly at it. Then Walter said,

'Your description of the moment of deconversion, when your central character realises how wrong he has been to trust the word of politicians rather than of honest imaginative writers like Gide, is one of the most moving things I have ever read. It reminded me of that last verse we used to be so excited by in Baudelaire's poem about the great painters where he says that art is the best testimony human beings can give of their dignity.' Suddenly Walter, in very English French – or Anglo-American French – and without raising or lowering his voice, spoke the lines,

' "Car c'est vraiment, Seigneur, le meilleur témoignage
Que nous puissions donner de notre dignité." '

There was an irony in his tone, implying perhaps that he no longer thought art quite as important as he and Arnold had once believed it to be, but the lines would almost have brought nostalgic tears into Arnold's eyes if his attention hadn't been abruptly diverted to a group of three youngish head-scarved and Fair Isle jumpered women sitting at a table near the bar. They were looking at Walter less with disapproval than with embarrassed concern, as though they suspected him of being a patient allowed out for the day from a mental hospital. They might be connected with the four yachtsmen at the bar, who were taking little notice of them however and also were giving the impression – which was likely to be a pretence – of not having heard Walter speaking French verse. But Arnold's uncomfortable awareness of the women and the yachtsmen did not make him forget his unease about Walter's apparent assumption that he had completely rejected his former left-wing views. At last, although he was very reluctant to risk lessening Walter's admiration for his book, he said,

'My disillusionment with Stalin didn't mean I became disillusioned with Marx or with Lenin.'

'I guessed that from your book. You obviously have quite a way to go yet before realising that there must have been something in Lenin, and in Marx too, which was bound to lead to an autocracy like Stalin's.' Walter's assertively authoritative tone caused no uneasiness in Arnold, who remembered how habitually Walter had spoken like this forty years ago when arguing about anything he considered important: and Arnold was glad that Walter seemed not to have formed his high opinion of the book in unawareness of its Leninism. Arnold said,

'Lenin can hardly be blamed for being revised and distorted by Stalin, any more than for being completely repudiated by Euro-Communists now.'

'If you think as you apparently do in your book that almost every existing communist party has gone "revision-ist" ' – Walter's emphasis on this word seemed to imply a criticism of it – 'how can you claim that the teachings of

Marx and Lenin have any practical importance any longer in the world at all?'

'I believe there is bound to be a revival of Leninist Marxism,' Arnold said with an assertiveness something like Walter's. 'As world capitalism in its deepest crisis yet becomes more and more repressive and heads towards nuclear war, the working class will see through their reformist leaders and will join the revolutionaries who want to get rid of capitalism.'

Arnold's voice had become louder but he didn't know it had until he saw one of the yachtsmen – with darkly red cheeks and a handlebar moustache which Arnold in other circumstances might have found comic rather than ugly – staring openly and hostilely at him. Walter showed no consciousness of the stare, and Arnold tried to seem unconscious of it too. Walter said,

'The working class when it becomes disillusioned with reformists is much more likely to turn to fascism than to Leninism. Proletarian revolution was one of our least clever hopes in the 'thirties.'

'An anti-imperialist revolution has already begun in the Third World,' Arnold said, 'and whatever mistakes the workers in the imperialist countries may yet make they will ally themselves with it at last.'

'So you're hoping for a revolution still,' Walter loudly said, 'though no doubt you wouldn't disagree with Marx and Engels that class struggle has sometimes led to the common ruin of the contending classes, and presumably you've realised there could be final ruin this time.'

'There could be, but this will depend on whether or not the revolutionary movement can get sufficient support to break the power of capitalism before capitalism can destroy us all,' Arnold said not so loudly. He could not refrain from adding, 'The revolution needs support from poets too.'

'Auden was entirely right when he pointed out that poets didn't save a single Jew from the gas chambers,' Walter said, 'and he was right too in saying that a poet shouldn't be expected to come out with public statements about politics any more than a dustman should.'

'Auden wasn't being politically neutral when he made those two public statements,' Arnold said. 'He was helping the imperialists who want poetry to be silent about their crimes.'

Walter suddenly stood up, saying,

'I'm afraid I'll have to go to the lats.' He used their old word for it. 'I think I've got a touch of summer diarrhoea.' He added, as if to make clear that there was no connection between it and his conversation with Arnold, 'I suspected it after breakfast this morning.'

He glanced around the bar-room for a moment or two. Then like a homing pigeon that had found its bearings he went straight towards the end of the bar where the red-faced handlebar-moustached yachtsman stood glaring at him. Walter appeared to be about to speak to the yachtsman but actually he was looking well above the man's head at a pointed wooden sign with *Toilets* printed in gilt letters along it. He walked on, seemingly not noticing the man who glaringly watched him disappear through a doorway to the left of the bar, and who continued to watch the doorway for almost a minute after Walter's disappearance; but when the yachtsman gave up watching he turned to face the bar again, not to stare at Arnold. Evidently he was less resentful and suspicious of Arnold than of Walter.

Arnold sitting alone in the shadowy alcove soon began to regret more and more that he had been talking with Walter about things that divided them instead of trying to tell him how deeply he still admired his poetry. 'If I had not been his friend and known him as a living poet,' Arnold thought, 'I would never have known how marvellous human life at its best can be.' This was what Arnold needed to tell Walter, and would tell him as soon as he came back to the alcove. But Walter was taking a long time to come back. Arnold, looking towards the doorway through which Walter had disappeared, was all at once conscious that the yachtsman with the handlebar moustache was no longer standing at the bar. The man might have followed Walter out of the bar-room and might be physically attacking him now. An apprehensiveness grew in Arnold as minutes passed and neither of them reappeared. He got up and walked across to the bar and then through the open doorway towards the toilets.

He found himself in an even narrower and darker passageway than the one by which he and Walter had come into the bar-room from the street. There were two doors along the lefthand side of the passage, and on the first of these Arnold was able to read the word *Wenches* inscribed in black lettering with a facetiously antique double V instead of a W. He opened the second door, hardly glancing at the similarly pseudo-antique inscription on it, which looked something like *Gallants*, and he came into a white-tiled Gents lavatory where a large man was standing alone at the urinals with his back to the door. It was the yachtsman. Walter must be in one of the three closets on the opposite side of the room. He might have become ill, perhaps ill enough to be incapable of getting out of the closet he was in. Arnold thought of going to listen at one or other of the closet doors, but he realised that if he were to do this it would almost certainly be noticed by the yachtsman who might assume it was some sort of obscene perversion and might compensate for his failure to beat-up Walter by beating-up Arnold instead – and the same could happen if Arnold did nothing yet except stand here waiting for him to go away. So Arnold went and stood at the urinals, though as far as possible from the yachtsman, the whole upper half of whose body now appeared to be gradually swelling up, as if he was drawing an immensely deep breath or had become tumescent with rage. At last the man buttoned up his flies and walked away to go out into the passage, morosely ignoring Arnold, who as soon as he had gone moved quickly over to the closets. Surprised that the engaged sign was not showing on any of their doors, Arnold opened the nearest of these. Walter was not inside, nor in the next closet, nor the third. Then just beyond the closets Arnold found a larger doorway already open, and he walked out of this into a yard which had wild plants growing between its flagstones and was enclosed on three sides by the windowed and balconied walls of the inn building, and in the middle of the fourth side there was an archway that led into the street. This was the route that Walter must have taken, Arnold thought, as he himself walked across the yard and through the archway. But why hadn't Walter come back into the inn by the front entrance from the street?

Might he have missed the entrance by turning to the right instead of to the left when he had come out through the archway? Arnold stood looking up and down the street, which was quite crowded now, probably with people who had disembarked from the next ferry-boat after the one Walter had arrived by, and he was unable to see anyone who could be Walter. He decided to walk down the street to the right, against the main movement of the crowd. Without meeting Walter he reached the quay, from which the ferry-boat was just beginning to move away. A black-jerseyed man had lifted the noose of a thick rope from a bollard at the edge of the quay, and at the stern of the boat another man was operating a capstan to bring the rope on board. Arnold was about to turn round with the idea of going back past the inn to search for Walter along the street to the left of the entrance, but his attention was caught by something he thought he saw, and then was certain he saw, on the ferry-boat. It was Walter's alkanet-blue light summer jacket.

Walter was there on the deck among the other passengers. He was looking towards Arnold, without seeing him. The shock Arnold felt gave way after a moment to the bitterest remorse. His guess was that by criticising Auden he had given deadly offence to Walter who must have suspected rightly enough that the criticism was aimed at himself too. But when the boat began to move at full speed away from the quay Walter suddenly did see Arnold and smiled and waved to him as if nothing in the least untoward had happened. Arnold smiled and waved back, sure now that whatever unguessable reason Walter had had for so abruptly leaving him it didn't mean that the ending of their long estrange-ment had been illusory. They remained looking and smiling at each other as the boat moved farther away, until a cloud-shadow passed over the deck, momentarily causing Walter's face to seem even more saggingly and horrifying old than in Arnold's dream two nights before, but Walter became younger again when the shadow had gone, though soon his features were indistinct in the renewed sunlight as the boat took him still farther from Arnold and nearer to the dark-treed overclouded mainland.

The Night Walk

AN OLD MAN got out of bed in the dark and went to his bedroom window to convince himself that a huge explosion during the nightmare he had just woken from had not been real. Through the intact glass of the large sash-window pane he stared down at a street lit by unshattered street lamps as well as by a gibbous moon low in the sky, and he saw no movement at all there. He heard no noises either, no sirens of police cars or fire-engines or ambulances. Yet he could not quickly free his consciousness from what he had dreamed he had seen after hearing the explosion: at the far end of a short side-street a façadeless moonlit building had shown an interior in which a horse with its head flayed and skinlessly glistening stood untotteringly upright, while around it like a maimed spider a white-toothed bleedingly lipless ape capered on all fours in agony with its belly uppermost, and the blue-overalled slaughterman whose work the explosion had interrupted lay face down on the blood-spattered floor of the building. The old man, continuing to look out at the real street empty and quiet below his window, was unable to become totally sure of the unreality of the abattoir scene until he was sufficiently awake to remember the actual external danger that had been the cause of all his recent nightmares, though this was invisible and inaudible to him at present.

Something of it was soon audible and then visible. He heard a faraway thunderlike rumble which grew gradually louder and became a roar in the night sky immediately overhead. A monstrous low-flying aeroplane with red lights winking was about to land at one of the many military air bases owned and controlled throughout the country by a foreign imperialist power. After it had gone out of sight he looked up at the constellation Orion which it had temporarily eclipsed and he tried to calm himself by testing his memory of the names of the brighter stars there. Every autumn when night skies were darker than in summer he had a habit of repeating star names to himself so that old age should not make him forget them, just as each spring he repeated the names of the wild flowers he saw. But naming Betelgeuse and Bellatrix and Rigel could not deaden the rage this loud aeroplane had revived in him against the occupying forces and against all the successive governments here which had servilely welcomed their presence, nor could he get philosophic peace from the thought that long after the possible nuclear destruction of most of the human race the positions of the stars in Orion would appear more or less the same to an observer on earth as they did to him tonight. If he had been younger, or even if he hadn't so recently been seriously ill, he might have had the courage to go down at once into the streets now and to do what he had for so long wished he could do – try to make contact with members of the resistance movement. How ironic it was, he thought as he turned from the window to go back to his bed, that the old with at most only a few years, probably of ill health, to look forward to were so much less ready than the young to take risks that might cause them to lose their lives. But after getting back into bed he felt too restlessly ashamed of himself to be able to sleep and he soon got out again and quickly dressed himself in his daytime clothes. He quietly opened the bedroom door, and quietly also he went down the stairs, though as no one else was in the house his cautiousness wasn't necessary yet. There was more point to it when, after reaching the hall below and putting on his outdoor shoes and his anorak and his corduroy cap, he slowly opened the front door. Any noise made by that could have been heard in the street.

He stood outside for a while with his hand on the handle of the still not quite shut door behind him and looked up and down the street without seeing anyone about. He began to walk along the pavement in the direction of the docks. If he was unlucky enough to be stopped by officers of the National Political Police in a patrol car all he could do would be to explain that he was taking this walk because he suffered from insomnia. But in actuality he walked on for two or three minutes without meeting anyone. He was approaching a side-street which although he was not yet near enough to the entrance of it to be able to see down it very far reminded him – he didn't know why – of the side-street in his nightmare. Perhaps the light from that had shafted out across the main-street as strongly as it did here, so strongly here that the light of the main-street now seemed penumbral compared with it. Two shadows, squat and sharp-edged, jutted suddenly out from the side-street and were rapidly elongated till they became two men wearing black uniforms who rushed directly at the old man, and then as if he were invisible – in the way that the old sometimes are to the less old – though not only invisible but intangible also, they passed straight through him.

He knew almost at once that these must be the shadows of the men, – not yet the men themselves, who however would follow their shadows at any moment. He was lucky to be very near a recessed doorway beside the pavement, and he managed to make a short leap sideways into the darkness of the recess. Moving with long fast strides the two men went by, not seeming to notice where he had gone. But someone else was already here. A woman. She gave no sign of fright. She said quietly, 'They'll be back soon. You'd better come in with me.'

She took a latch key from a small fancy hand-bag which was attached by a looped cord to her wrist and as she reached up to put the key into the key-hole he saw that there was a large pompom on her wrist such as a clown might wear and that her sleeve was made of net-like material through which the flesh of her arm showed. She opened the door and switched on a dim light. He followed her into the hall passage-way and to the foot of the staircase there. She began to go up the stairs, glancing back for a moment to make sure he was still following her. She wore a bulkily thick fluffy-haired black coat that covered her shoulders and rose to her neck but was sleeveless and reached down no lower than her buttocks, below which her fine-mesh black net stockings or tights had a pinkish grey look because of the flesh visible through them, and there were large black pompoms on her stilt-heeled shoes. The likeness that her get-up gave her to a shaved poodle was emphasised by her mincingly prancing steps, necessary perhaps because of her exceptionally high heels, as she mounted the stairs. On the landing at the top of the stairs she said to him,

'I am a Red too.'

She seemed to be inviting him to confirm that he was one, but mistrust of her kept him silent.

'Perhaps you wouldn't expect a revolutionary to work as a common prostitute,' she said.

She opened a door half-way along the landing and switched on a light to show a room containing tassle-fringed and luridly patterned soft furnishings of such potent vulgarity that he felt they could only have been chosen by someone artistically sensitive who had knowingly aimed at achieving an effect of extreme tastelessness.

'This is my working boudoir,' she said. Then she led him farther along the passage to another door which she opened, saying, 'This is my living room. Make yourself as comfortable as you can here. I'll come and explain myself as soon as I've changed out of my working clothes.'

She left him. He looked around him for somewhere to sit. The room was like a junk shop, filled with various mainly ornamental objects though with some useful ones, but seemingly no chairs. There was a divan, however, placed alongside one of the walls. It had cushions at each end of it which he suspected might be pillows with daytime covers over them, and the divan might be a disguised bed already made-up with sheets and blankets. He sat down on the edge of it. He had the thought that she might be telephoning the police now to say she'd got him trapped here. But why should she be doing that when she could so easily have left him to be seized by them in the street? He began looking at objects in the room with a vague hope of finding clues to her character. From the wall beside the fireplace a fretworked Swiss cuckoo clock hung with its pendulum swinging. Just clear of its chain-suspended iron weights was a gas cooker, close to which he saw an old earthen-ware kitchen sink, and from the corner of the room near to this and extending along another wall was a big table loaded with more things than he could have taken detailed note of in under ten minutes even if he'd got up and gone to the table. He saw a plaster bust and a bronze head, an art nouveau wash basin and jug with a pattern of curving purple trees beneath their shining glaze, a collection of large beach stones, an antler-like tree branch barklessly white, an aitch bone, a stuffed falcon in a domed glass case. He saw painter's canvases piled against the wall near the door. He saw, sooner than he had expected, the woman who had called herself a prostitute come back through the door into the room.

She was wearing a dark green roll-necked pullover and dark brown corduroy trousers. She had changed her stilt-heeled shoes for heel-less mocassin-like slippers. She had even found time to tone down the bright make-up he was sure he remembered seeing on her face.

'You'll be safe here,' she said. 'They won't come into the house.'

'Why won't they?'

'Because I have a Protector who is a V.I.P. from the ministry for Home Defence. He's one of the deadliest of the whole top gang, but I am able to use him to better purpose than he uses me. Though you may not trust me yet – and I can't blame you if you don't – I'm going to trust you enough to tell you I've succeeded in getting quite a few items of information out of him which have been useful to the Resistance.'

She came and sat down on the divan at the other end of it from where he was sitting. He said,

'Isn't there a risk of his getting information out of you?'

'I am a socialist and I am one hundred per cent for the Resistance,' she said. 'I don't know how I would behave under torture, but he's become too dependent on my professional services to want to put me to that test yet, and he's heard nothing about the Resistance from me.'

The old man did not comment, feeling distrustful of her still. She went on,

'I am a socialist because of my experiences as a prostitute, and I am a prostitute because I could see no alternative that wasn't worse. And the reason I'm telling you all this is that I think you are a socialist too. You are, aren't you?'

He avoided giving her a direct answer. He asked,

'What made you guess I might be a socialist?'

'The police were after you and you don't give the impression of being a "common criminal".'

Her emphasis on this phrase seemed meant to show her dislike for it and indicated a degree of social and political sensitivity in her which surprised him. But it also revived an earlier doubt he had had about her truthfulness.

'You don't give the impression of being a "common prostitute", as you called yourself,' he said.

'Did I? I must have been thinking of my visit this evening to a client of mine who likes me to pretend I am. He likes to pick me up in the street as if he'd never seen me before. When you found me at my front door I had just come back from his luxury flat. He's well-heeled, as the rest of my clients also are, and I make myself expensive for them so that I don't have to have too many of them and I can get some leisure in my life.'

'You give the impression of coming from a well-heeled family yourself. Your voice and your use of language seem very middle-class. And yet you say you became a prostitute because you had no alternative.'

'I was an adopted child and my adoptive parents were upper middle-class with liberal ideas. They named me Aminta. They sent me to state schools. At my Comprehensive I had a boy friend who was three years older than me and called himself a Nihilist. He believed that all teachers are capitalist agents and that it's natural for all children to revolt against their parents. He said we should aim to disrupt the school. He left and went abroad and I didn't see him again. I truanted a lot and never took any exams, though I could have done well at them, especially in art. Then I ran away from "home". I got a job in a small factory, a real sweat-shop. I decided I would rather be a prostitute. That's how it all began.'

He could almost believe her story. But he asked,

'Didn't your upper middle-class adoptive parents take any steps to get you brought back to them?'

'No. Long before I ran away they already knew they couldn't cope with me. They were no longer young when they adopted me. That was a large part of the trouble. And now they are both dead.'

Aminta moved to sit farther back on the divan and a little nearer to him.

'My only real home now is my Art,' she said.

'What art?' he asked.

'I paint. I am an artist in my spare time. I should be glad if you would let me show you some of my pictures. May I?'

'Yes,' he could only say.

She went over to the canvases stacked against the wall near the door. She pulled out one of them and brought it to him to look at.

'This is an early one, in my modernist style which I've given up now.'

He saw an a-symmetrical pattern of pale yellow human hands against an evenly coloured yellow-brown background. Their fingers and thumbs were mere stumps, as in those cave paintings of fifteen thousand years ago where the outlined shapes of actual human hands, similarly mutilated, had been stencilled on the rock-walls. He did not much like the picture, but he thought it could be the work of someone genuinely trying to be a serious artist. Suddenly, though he still could not help doubting whether she had been wholly truthful in the story she had told him about herself, he felt safer in this house with her than he had been able to feel before.

'It's an extraordinary painting,' he said; and partly to avoid having to comment on it further he asked, 'What does your Protector think of it?'

'He is condescendingly tolerant of it and of the few other

paintings of mine I've let him see, but there's one thing he really does admire about me as an artist and that is the artistic cunning he says I've perversely shown in my deliberate choice of such supremely inartistic furnishings for my boudoir. He is greatly amused by that – and stimulated. It helps to turn him on, the swine.'

As she didn't appear to resent the old man's question about her Protector, he asked one more about him, though it had nothing to do with her painting; 'Doesn't he object to your having other clients besides himself?'

'He does at times and at times he doesn't. I've got him under control. But let's forget him now.'

She took back the canvas to the stack and brought out another one.

'This is in my transitional style – half-way between modernism and post-modernism.'

At first sight it seemed to the old man an ordinary enough modernist abstract. Some of the colours were Turneresque, he thought – sunset crimsons, and smoky browns, yellows and blues; and in the lower half of the picture there were triangular shapes resembling the sails of yachts.

'How is this transitional?' he asked.

'The idea of it came to me from an actual scene at the sea-side last summer,' she said, 'whereas the hands came by accident while I was doodling – "taking a line for a walk" as Paul Klee would have said.'

'Are these sails?' He pointed to the triangles.

'The shapes were suggested to me one afternoon while I was on the pier watching a few small catamarans and windsurfers which were scudding over the water with amazing speed, skidding like toboggans on ice, then bucking and rocking, or becoming suddenly becalmed. But this isn't a picture *of* anything. It isn't representational.'

'And what suggested these two shapes like truncated

149

cones with crescents under them here above the sail-like shapes?'

'I saw two broad-funnelled tugs near the pier, both of them unusually large, not dirty as tugs often are, one of them with a pale blue hull and a dark reddish-lilac funnel – like a "truncated cone" as you say – and the other's funnel had the same shape but its colour was a light lemon yellow above a deeper than emerald green hull which had a shine on it like the shine of water.'

Her description made the picture look better to him than he had found it at first. But he asked, 'And was there a larger boat somewhere on the horizon with a structure like a small-scale Eiffel tower rising out of it?'

'How did you know?' she said, surprised.

'I didn't, but that's what the derricks for oil drills sometimes look like, and your seeing such a boat means that those tugs were helping to prospect for oil.'

'I knew they were.'

'If it's found there the whole holiday scene could be blighted for miles and for years.'

'I knew that too, of course, but the picture was suggested to me by the exciting colours of the funnels and the hulls – not by the function of the tugs.'

'And didn't your knowing their function have any effect on how you saw their colours?'

'Perhaps the contrast between the marvellousness of the colours and the ugliness of what the tugs might help to do made the colours all the more exhilarating to me.'

'The colours were meant to lure the public into believing that the oil company's operations would never smirch the beauty of the scene.' He became aware that he might be wounding her feelings and also that he wanted to avoid doing this. He went on, not quite truthfully, 'Of course I'm not implying there's anything in the least deceitful about your picture. I do understand it's not representational. Its colours are very striking, I think.'

'I certainly didn't paint it to advertise the oil company,' she said, and he thought, 'Or to expose the company's real intentions either.' He said,

'I should like to see some of your post-modernist work.'

She returned to the stack to change the tugs picture for one which looked like a painted imitation of a coloured photograph. It showed a young woman wearing a pale green dress and standing bare-legged on the bright yellow sands of a seaside beach with her arm raised in the act apparently of throwing a dove-white seagull towards a child who stood with outstretched hands a short distance away from her.

'This was my first post-modernist attempt,' Aminta said. 'I painted it soon after finishing my tugs picture, during the same summer holiday.'

'It's very naturalistic, yet the girl's throwing of the seagull is obviously imaginary and shows that the picture isn't just a copy from life.'

She seemed pleased by his comment, which was intended to please her. 'No, it's not a copy but it was suggested by something I actually saw. The real woman on the beach lifted her arm to throw a tennis ball to the child, but what appeared to leave her hand as she threw wasn't the ball – it was a gull which happened to fly past on a level with her extended arm at that moment.'

'A surrealist film director would have been glad to have thought up a happening like that,' he said. 'Of course I do recognise that your picture aims at being more than merely startling and incongruous. It isn't surrealistic.'

She looked pleased, until he asked,

'Is it symbolic?'

'No. Why do you ask?'

'Because of the dove-white seagull.'

'This is a black-headed gull, not a cliché peace symbol, if that's what you're thinking.'

'I'm sorry. I hadn't noticed how dark the gull's head was.'

He felt a momentary slight faintness. He must have become too hot in this room. He undid his anorak at the top. She said,

'Why don't you take it off?'

He unzipped his anorak and laid it on the divan beside his corduroy cap which he had put there after she had left him by himself in the room. He shifted farther back on the divan from his hitherto upright position near its edge and his elbows sank into the cushion behind him. She went to put the gull canvas back in the stack and returned to sit on the divan again, nearer to him than before. She said,

'I don't think art ought to be politically propagandist.'

He was goaded into saying,

'That seems a very old-hat modernist idea. There may be many perfectly sincere and politically active socialists who have fallen for it, but I think it is quite illogical – and unsocialist.'

'Art is ineffective as a weapon, compared with direct political activity.'

'Perhaps, but politically propagandist art can at least give some help to the struggle.'

'The harder the struggle becomes the less politically effective art will be,' she said.

He thought of saying that the communist leaders of the successful revolutions in Russia and China would not have agreed with that, but he was feeling increasingly disinclined to argue with her. Nevertheless when she went on, 'And art used as a weapon becomes crude and inferior as art,' he did say,

'That need not happen.'

'You know it does happen. Politics denatures art, and war

which is "a continuation of politics by other means" literally destroys works of art and artists too.'

She moved closer to him on the divan.

'Art is gladness,' she said. 'Political conflict isn't. I am not being escapist. I don't doubt that the victory of the revolution is the first necessity if art is to survive and to come fully into its own.'

He found that she had moved still closer to him and that he had allowed himself to sink farther back into the cushion behind him.

'Art is the only paradise there will ever be on earth,' she said.

He did not say anything. They lay back on the divan, neither of them speaking. They were very close to each other, though there was no physical contact between them. He became sure that before long there would be, and that he did not want to avoid it. But startlingly the front door bell rang downstairs. Three times, in extremely quick succession.

'It's him,' she said, getting up from the divan. 'The swine. He's never arrived here before without phoning me first. Stay where you are until I've got him into the boudoir.' She moved towards the door of the room, saying, 'As soon as you hear the beginning of a loud pop disc I shall play to him on my record-player there, leave the house at once.'

She switched off the light of the room as she went out to the landing, but she did not shut the door. Perhaps she thought her visitor would be less likely to be suspicious if he saw it wasn't shut. The old man heard her go downstairs and open the front door and he heard a rather high-pitched but not angry male voice. He noticed that the light from the landing was shining into the room and that though dim it was shining on the divan and on him. He stood up with the idea of moving out of the light; then, realising the risk of knocking noisily against some shadowy art object in the room, he sat down on the divan again and made himself as still as he could just in time before Aminta followed by her 'Protector' – as the old man assumed him to be – came to the top of the stairs and on to the landing. She kept ahead of her Protector, thereby screening the open doorway from his view but also obstructing the old man's view of him, and guided him into the boudoir before her. The only impression the old man got from what little the tall interposed figure of Aminta allowed to be seen of this important person was that he was slim and short and wore a grey suit not a uniform.

It seemed a long time before the old man heard the pop music start up from Aminta's record-player inside the boudoir. The sound was both loud and sensually yearning, as though she had turned up the volume of a song of the nineteen twenties or thirties which the singer had meant to be seductively soft. The old man, hurriedly putting on his anorak and his corduroy cap, moved as quickly and as quietly as he could out of the room and past the closed door of the boudoir and rather less quickly and even more carefully down the stairs. He opened the front door hesitantly, remembering there was danger outside as well as in. But he saw nobody about when he stepped into the street.

He found himself beginning to walk back in the direction of his own house, without having consciously decided to do so. He would not have far to go. He couldn't yet see his house, though the street ahead of him was very straight and in the gap between high buildings on either side of the distant end of it the large gibbous moon, lower than the tops of the buildings, gave out at least as much light as the street lamps in their two converging and far-reaching but never meeting rows along the pavements. And still there was no sign of anybody about, nor was there any traffic. He thought this might be because of the time of night (or rather of morning) which he guessed, from his memory of the position of Orion as viewed by him through his south-facing bedroom window probably less than an hour ago, was around three o'clock. The slightly rising slope of the street along its whole length ahead towards the setting moon made the pavements at the base of even the farthest building visible to him. He could now clearly see the front door of his house. He stopped walking. Why was he going back there? He had shamefully allowed his talk with Aminta to make him forget his purpose of trying to get in touch with the Resistance. Abruptly he turned round and began walking once more in the direction he had taken when he had left his house – towards the docks.

He thought as he walked that in the act of turning he had glimpsed a movement of shadows on the pavement quite near his front door. Within two or three minutes he heard men's voices far behind him, two voices, raucously singing. The men must be drunk and were unlikely to be policemen, though they could attract the attention of policemen. They were some way behind him still when he came past Aminta's doorway and reached the nearby side-street. The light shafted as strongly as before from there across the main-street, but no squat sharp-edged shadows jutted suddenly out from the side-street. Nevertheless he slowed in his walk, hesitant to cross the light-beam that would brilliantly illuminate him for any policeman – or for the drunks behind him – to see. The drunks had become silent for a short while, but now their singing burst out much louder and nearer than before. They must have moved fast, remarkably fast for singing drunks. He turned quickly round the corner into the side-street, thinking that if he did this instead of continuing along the main street as he had intended, the beam would expose him for only an instant, if at all, to anyone coming up the main-street behind him. Soon after he had turned he believed he heard the singers go past the entrance of the side-street. Their singing stopped or became inaudible when they had passed. Only then was he aware again of the resemblance this street seemed to have to the side-street in his nightmare. What the resemblance exactly was he still didn't know. The large building at the end of the street was in the same position as the nightmare abattoir had been, but here its façade was undestroyed. However, adjacent to it there was a space half-covered with piles of rubble as if a small part of the building had been recently demolished. At the moment when he noticed this the singing of the drunks began again, very close behind him here in the side-street, not so raucous as before, and this time the words they sang were distinguishable:

'He's no bloody use to anyone,
He's no bloody use at all.'

They sang in unison, articulating the words very clearly. Then one of them said to the other, not at all drunkenly,

'Stop this. Mr Mitchell might think we mean him.'

They overtook the old man. They were both of them youngish-looking men, hatless, and both wore fawn-coloured belted raincoats. They came to a stop in front of him. The shorter of the two asked politely, almost deferentially,

'Are we right in guessing you are Mr Henry Mitchell?'

'Yes.' As they evidently knew he was, he felt there would be no point in pretending he wasn't.

'How extraordinary this is,' the taller said. 'I don't suppose you remember either of us, do you, sir?' There was no sneer in the way he said 'sir', nor was there deference; he spoke the word as if unthinkingly and as if it were a natural one to use in addressing Henry.

'No,' Henry said.

'You taught us both fifteen years ago at Condell's,' the shorter said. 'I'm Bowman.'

The three of them were standing almost directly beneath a street-lamp. Henry looked closely at Bowman, noting the pale blueness of his eyes and the even redness of his cheeks but especially the bigness of his neck which seemed more than half as broad as the whole breadth of the upper part of his body from shoulder to shoulder. The taller man, who had curly brown hair and a gaunt face with angular hollows under his cheek-bones, said,

'I'm Farrow.'

'I don't think I remember either of you.'

'His memory was never one of his stronger points,' Farrow said to Bowman, who however came to the defence of Henry:

'After more than thirty years at Condell's he could hardly be expected to remember everyone he tried to teach there.'

But Farrow persisted: 'We were in his form for a whole year and he couldn't put names to us by the end of it.'

'I can't believe that,' Henry said. 'I always made a point of learning the names of everyone in my form within the first week of term.'

'I'm sure you did,' Bowman said soothingly. 'And the big thing is that after fifteen years by great good chance we've met you again tonight. Farrow and I hadn't seen each other for quite a while either, and we were having a little celebration, weren't we, Farrow?'

'That's so,' Farrow said.

'We'd be very happy if you'd join us.'

'Perhaps he has another engagement,' Farrow said, and both of them looked keenly at Henry, who said,

'I don't sleep well. I went for a short walk and I was on my way home.'

'How come then that you've been walking away from your house for the last five minutes?' Farrow asked, and without waiting for Henry to think up an answer he said to Bowman,

'I wonder if he could have been going to one of those

meetings of the kind he used to creep out to nearly every evening after a day's teaching.'

'Oh no. I'm sure old Miffy must have given all that up ages ago. I daresay he's learnt a thing or two in his time about the disadvantages of extremist politics.'

Henry's nickname at the school had not been Miffy. It had been something rather more unpleasant – Missy. Bowman either knew this and was deliberately tempering his present insolence by inventing a nickname which might almost be affectionate, or if he didn't know it he could never have been taught by Henry, who anyway already suspected both him and Farrow of lying when they'd claimed they had been.

'I'm not so sure he's such a good learner,' Farrow said.

'Oh, he is, he is. And after all, he wasn't ever really enthusiastic about politics.' Bowman seemed eager to exculpate Henry.

'It's true he didn't become political for the sake of politics,' Farrow said. 'He only wanted to revenge himself on society for not having provided him with an easier job which he would have been as useless at as he was at teaching.'

'You're a bit hard on him. He wasn't quite hopeless as a teacher. You must admit he was conscientious – up to a point.'

'Yes, up to the point of making things just a little less uncomfortable for himself than they would have been if he had made no effort at all. And all the time he was inwardly seething with rage at his loss of freedom.'

'No, not all the time. I'm sure that by nature he was a mild enough little man, but understandably there were moments when he felt he could bear us no longer.'

Henry restrained himself from interrupting them. He knew he would merely increase his humiliation if he took part, no matter how angrily, in their talk about him. He turned round away from them and started walking towards the main street. In no time, they leapt after him and were standing in front of him again. They went on with their talk, ignoring him as before.

'Those outbursts of his in class were quite frightening,' Farrow said. 'Perhaps all the more so because they didn't seem to be aimed particularly against any of us. He hardly looked at us as he yelled. It was as if he was attacking the whole universe.'

'They were effective. None of us liked his rages. None of us tried to provoke him into them deliberately.'

'They didn't help me to take any interest in the work I had to produce for him. He was a complete mess and misfit as a teacher.'

'You're not being fair to him, Farrow. At the first school where he ever taught he was so keen that he used to spend the whole of his half-term holidays planning his work for the rest of the term.'

Although this was more or less true, Henry was sure that Bowman could not possibly have been told of it, as no one except Henry himself knew of it. Bowman was merely making a guess, an unpleasantly astute guess. Farrow said,

'The iron must have entered his soul pretty soon after that.'

'I just don't believe that either of you were ever taught by me,' Henry said angrily. He turned his back on them.

'He's the old Miffy still,' Bowman said.

Henry walked away from them. They did not immediately follow him, but went on talking, no doubt about him. He did not hear what they were saying. He was approaching the large building that faced him with its broad undemolished façade at the end of this side-street. He was within ten yards of the building before he realised that the street was a cul-de-sac. He went towards a door in the façade. He thought of knocking on it and asking to be given refuge from two men who were harassing him. He came to a stop in front of the door. He heard a short sardonically contemptuous laugh behind him, some way behind him. Bowman and Farrow must have remained standing where they had been when he had left them. The door had no knocker or handle on it and there was a six-inch gap below the bottom of it – perhaps to allow slaughter-house blood to come rilling out over the pavement into the gutter, he momentarily let himself imagine. He heard Farrow's sardonic laugh – it certainly was Farrow's – behind him again, though no nearer yet. He pushed the door, which opened easily and swung back after him as he stepped into a glass-roofed concrete-floored passage lit mainly by the street lamplight shining through the gap beneath the door. Halfway along one side of the passage there was another door, also without a handle or knocker but with a Yale lock. He thumped on this door several times with the heel of his hand. Then Farrow followed by Bowman came abruptly into the passage from the street.

'He's fantasising,' Farrow said. 'He's dreaming of being invited in for the night by some gerontophiliac young widow with advanced ideas and refined artistic tastes.'

'I hope he won't be too disappointed to discover it's our town mansion he happens to have arrived at,' Bowman said. 'All of his own accord too.'

Farrow pushed a key into the Yale lock and opened the door.

'In you go, old Miffy,' Bowman said, contemptuously emphasising the nickname and giving Henry a firm shove from behind.

Henry found himself inside what seemed to be a large diffusely lit gymnasium with ropes hanging from overhead beams, and alongside one of the walls he saw parallel bars and a horizontal bar.

'Would you mind letting me go home,' he said, as coolly as he could.

'That's not where you were going when we first caught sight of you,' Farrow said.

'I was going there before I noticed you coming towards me in the distance. Soon afterward I was walking in the opposite direction.'

'Why?' Farrow asked sharply.

'You were noisy and I thought you were drunks who might be violent.'

'When you started out from your house tonight you were on your way to a political meeting, weren't you?' Farrow said.

'No.'

'Shall we let him go?' Bowman suggested. 'After all, he has always been just as useless at politics as he was at teaching. He's done more damage in his time to the subversive cause he tried to help than he could ever have done to the state he wanted to overthrow.'

'That's true enough,' Farrow said. 'He couldn't even be loyal to the vile Party he joined.'

'This ought to be counted in his favour.'

'He's treacherous by nature, and anyone who plans treason however impotently must be made to suffer for it.'

'He has suffered for it,' Bowman said with pseudo-sympathy. 'He has been poisoned by it for years.'

Farrow said directly to Henry, 'Who were you going to meet tonight?'

'No one. As I've already told you, I went out because I could not sleep.'

'Do you know where you are now?' Bowman asked.

'How could I? I only know I'm here against my will.'

'You are in a place of interrogation,' Farrow said. 'And I may as well tell you we are Intelligence agents. Who were you going to meet?'

'No one.'

'We have a horse here,' Farrow said.

'There's no need to be really nasty to him,' Bowman said, in a seemingly pleading tone. 'He's a reasonable little man and he'll co-operate without that. Won't you, Miffy?'

Henry hardly heard the question. The flayed horse he had seen in his nightmare and the maimed ape capering around the horse came vividly into his mind, but the face of the ape as he saw it now in his imagination had become human, and was recognisably his own face.

'We have a horse,' Farrow repeated.

He stepped aside from his position in front of Henry, who was enabled to see at the far end of the gymnasium a shinily brown leather-covered vaulting horse with its legs rigid like those of the untottering horse in his nightmare.

A bell began to ring, loudly, high-pitched like an alarm bell, but with brief intervals in its ringing as if it came from a telephone, which it did, and Bowman went over to a near corner of the gymnasium where the telephone was. After a brief conversation which on his part consisted of two phrases only, the first being 'Yes sir' which he repeated several times and the last being 'At once, sir,' he hung up the receiver on the wall hook he had taken it down from, and said morosely to Farrow,

'It's the Boss. We're to take Mitchell along immediately to Sir Howard Fasnet.'

'At this time of morning?' Farrow said with a resentment that seemed almost mutinous.

'Yes, and what's more the Boss says Sir Howard is extremely displeased at not being informed that we've brought Mitchell here.'

'That's the Boss's fault, not ours.'

Farrow turned angrily on Henry and seizing him violently by the arm jerked him round and forward towards the door of the gymnasium, saying,

'Come on, you geriatric slob.'

Bowman seized Henry's other arm in an even more painful grip, and when they'd got him out into the glass-roofed passage-way it was Bowman who punched him in the stomach. Henry doubled up, winded.

'That's enough,' Farrow said. 'He must be in a presentable state when we get him to Sir Howard.'

They waited for Henry to recover his wind, then they pushed him out into the side-street through the swinging door with the six inch gap below it. But now in the street they no longer held his arms. Bowman walked beside him and Farrow close behind him. Bowman said,

'You can't imagine how lucky you've been.'

It was evident that Bowman, who earlier on had seemed a little less venomous than Farrow, was even more bitterly disappointed than Farrow at the thwarting of their intended interrogation of Henry, who could and did imagine, as he unwillingly walked on with them, how they might have used the horse to help them interrogate him. What he imagined made him almost unaware of the street, or of the direction in which they were taking him, or of the distance or duration of his walk with them, and neither of them spoke to him again until they brought him to a stop outside the front gate of a large Victorian house.

'You are going to see the Regional Commissioner for Home Defence,' Bowman then told him.

At each end of the front of the house, there was a yellow brick tower with a blue cone-shaped roof, and from the gate a gravel drive led half-way round a circular lawn to a porch which had yellow-brick crenellations above it. Inside the porch the front door, the upper part of which was glass with a spiky starlike pattern cut into it, swung open as if automatically like the door of a supermarket at the approach of a customer. Bowman walked in first and Henry was pushed in after him by Farrow. Then Henry was aware that the door had been opened not automatically but by a slim, white-haired middle-aged man, wearing a black wide-sleeved kimono-like dressing-gown, who entirely ignored Bowman and Farrow and said to him in a tone of the mildest politeness,

'I think you are Mr Henry Mitchell?'

Henry didn't answer, and the man went on,

'I am Sir Howard Fasnet.' After saying this he seemed to notice Bowman and Farrow for the first time, and he told them coldly,

'There will be no need for you here.'

They turned, and like whipped dogs they went out of the front door which he shut behind them. 'Come upstairs,' he said to Henry.

Henry followed him across a chandelier-lit Persian-carpeted hall to the staircase, and as they went up the stairs he saw that Fasnet wore grey trousers beneath his black dressing-gown. A short way along the broad passage at the top of the stairs a half-open door gave Henry a glimpse of a warmly lit brown room with leather-upholstered armchairs in it and with gilt-framed oil paintings hanging on its walls. It was like a room in an old-established London club, Henry thought. But Fasnet led him into another and very different room on the opposite side of the passage. Here the chairs had tubular steel frames, and under bright strip lighting there were khaki-coloured steel filing cabinets rising high against the walls.

'This is where I do my homework as Minister for Home Defence,' Fasnet said. 'I've thought you might be less likely to suspect me of wanting to suborn you if I brought you in here rather than into my more sybaritically furnished sitting-room.'

Henry did not try to guess what he meant by 'suborn'. Fasnet, after sliding a steel-framed armchair towards Henry and then going behind a glass-topped desk to sit in a similar chair, went on to say,

'I feel I've known you for a long while, and not just through the usual channels by which I have to keep track of subversives in general.'

Henry remained standing and saying nothing.

'Do sit down,' Fasnet said unirritably. 'It will make me uncomfortable if you don't.'

Henry sat down.

'I first got to know you – or, more exactly, to know of you, but it has seemed almost as though I have always known you personally – thirty years ago, through a mutual friend of ours. Alfred Reaver. He was a colleague of yours at Condell's for a time wasn't he?' Fasnet did not wait for Henry to answer or to decline to answer. 'As you'll remember, he joined the ministry soon after the Second War. He was one of the pleasantest and ablest men I have ever met, and one of the least ambitious – which was just as well, because his association with you helped to prevent him from ever getting the promotion he deserved. Did you realise that?'

Henry would not answer.

'He never held it against you. He thought very highly of you. And though he disagreed with your opinions he did everything he could to protect you from the worst consequences that might otherwise have followed from the activities they led you into. There was even an occasion when he removed from our files a particularly damaging report on you, and "lost" it. Did you know that?'

'Reaver did not talk to me at all about his work at the ministry,' Henry said. He felt that Fasnet might be trying to get information out of him which could be used against Alfred, who could still be prosecuted though he had retired.

'Not at all?' Fasnet said. 'That was a pity. He could have amused you a lot if he had talked about it. He was a very amusing man. You should have heard him speaking over the phone at the ministry. We could always tell merely by his tone of voice the exact rank of whoever he happened to be speaking to. He took the micky out of even the highest, but so brilliantly that few of them suspected it and those who did couldn't resent it. However, it didn't really help his prospects of further promotion, any more than his efforts to protect you did.'

Henry was silent, and Fasnet said, 'I have protected you too.'

Henry stared at him. Fasnet's large eyes, widely spaced beneath a broad forehead, had a look of mild candour.

'I have protected you this evening. I am sorry I wasn't in time to stop those two official hoodlums from taking you to their gymnasium, but I did prevent them from doing their worst. It was a near thing. Two agents directly responsible to me had warned me that you had gone into Aminta's house, and I hoped to meet you with her, but she told me you weren't there, and what she tells me nowadays I find it convenient not to question.'

The revelation that Fasnet was Aminta's Protector did not now interest Henry, who asked with open disbelief,

'Why should you want to protect me?'

'Because I admire you.'

Henry, watching Fasnet's candid face, seemed to see satisfaction there, and he suspected he had let himself be lured into asking just the question that Fasnet had intended him to ask.

'I admire your persistence,' Fasnet said. 'I have kept myself informed of all your political activities since the war, both before and after you had to leave the Communist Party. I won't pretend I have ever shown the least sympathy for any

166

of the causes you have espoused, but I have been greatly impressed by your refusal to let your many disappointments get you down. First there was the Campaign for Nuclear Disarmament in its early phase, then the campaign against the American war in Vietnam' – Henry resisted an angry urge to object that neither of these, especially not the second, had been a disappointment – 'then there were a whole hotchpotch of other campaigns you gave your support to: against chemical and biological warfare, against the use of 245–T as a weedkiller in British forests, and the use of British troops in Northern Ireland, against racism in Britain and apartheid in South Africa and the exclusion of Palestinians from their own land, against pollution of the environment – and so on up to the campaign to prevent American nuclear missiles from being installed in this country. But perhaps your bitterest disappointment must have been the total failure of Unisoc, that non-party extra-parliamentary organisation you yourself thought up for bringing together all socialists who believe that the whole existing social and economic system needs to be fundamentally changed.'

Fasnet stopped, evidently expecting now that Henry would be provoked into making some comment, but he wasn't, and after a while Fasnet said,

'I admire your integrity still more than your persistence. You have undertaken these activities from a sense of duty to the human race and not because you had a liking or an aptitude for politics – you certainly hadn't – nor in the hope of advancing your career – you certainly didn't advance it, and even your political associates mostly didn't think all that highly of you.'

Henry said nothing. Fasnet tried a different approach:

'Hasn't it happened at least once recently that you have sat on the soft grass of a high hill in perfect weather and while you were looking at the countryside around you and down at

167

the glittering sea far below you the thought has come to you that neither this nor anything else in your life has been worth your having been born for?'

Henry tried to give no sign of his astonishment at the acuteness of Fasnet's guess. Or was it more than a guess? Had Henry described this actual experience of his in a letter which Fasnet's spies had made a copy of? Fasnet went on,

'Have you never said to yourself "If I knew that in ten minutes' time the whole human race, instantaneously and without any foreknowledge of what was coming or the least pain when it came, would be totally and finally exterminated, unless I pressed a button that could prevent this extermination – would I press the button?"?'

Henry could not stay silent any longer.

'If I ever asked myself such a question it could only have been because I had momentarily given way under the pressure of ruling ideas hostile to mine.'

Fasnet understood very well what Henry meant.

'My ideas are closer to yours than to the ideas of the ruling class I am a member of,' he said. 'You think of me as an anti-human monster, I dare say. Yet my aims are the same as yours, though my methods are other than yours, and far more effective. You believe in battling against the stream, whereas I go with it, and help it to go faster. I zealously support the extremist policies favoured by the most re-actionary of my ministerial colleagues – policies which will lead them and the whole capitalist system most rapidly to disaster and will hasten the victory of the working people of the world.'

Henry looked at Fasnet with distrustful amazement, and said,

'Those policies could destroy the human race.'

'They could, but that's unlikely, I think. I am an optimist, and so should you be – if you're a Marxist.'

'In helping to implement such policies you are responsible for horrible cruelties.'

'Yes, I am,' Fasnet admitted, not seeming to resent Henry's accusation, 'and I deeply regret it. However, I'm not naïve, and I realise that the great cause you and I both support can never triumph unless its leaders recognise the necessity sometimes of sacrificing a few hundred of its supporters in order to annihilate many thousands of its counter-revolutionary enemies. But I try to moderate my cruelties – in so far as I can do so without arousing any suspicion among my colleagues that I'm what they repulsively call a "wet".'

Henry said nothing.

'You are horrified and disgusted by what I'm telling you,' Fasnet went on. 'I can see that. And I honour you for it. I too want to put an end to all cruelty among human beings. The difference between us is that my methods, besides being more likely than yours to expedite the coming of revolution, have won me the mistaken approval of people in power and enabled me to live for pleasure in my spare time, whereas yours have caused you to live a life verging always on failure and sometimes on despair. Isn't it time you tried to get a little happiness out of life?'

Henry would not answer.

'I'm not trying to suggest that you should assist me in my home defence duties,' Fasnet said, 'only that you should take a deserved rest from your socialist activities at last and be content to let capitalism go its own way to destruction while you enjoy yourself as best you still can, intellectually – yes, and physically too.'

'I could never be happy if I connived at capitalism's crimes.'

'I expected you to say that. I would even have been disappointed in you if you hadn't. You would have been untrue to yourself. I only wanted to make things as easy as I can for you, and I will still do that. I will see to it that you are not molested by the so-called forces of order when you leave this house – or followed by them either, wherever you may choose to go.'

Fasnet stood up from the chair behind his desk.

'I think you had better leave now,' he said, 'before the next bomb scare. Did you guess there had been a warning tonight that a very large bomb had been placed in a building between here and your home?'

'No.'

'I would have thought you would have noticed that the traffic had been stopped.' Fasnet looked closely at Henry, who said nothing. 'But the warning seems to have been a hoax.' Fasnet moved away from his desk and towards the door of the room, and Henry was aware of being expected to follow him as he went out into the passage.

When they began going down the stairs to the hall the suspicion grew in Henry that Fasnet's declared aim of helping the revolution by pursuing extremist counter-revolutionary policies was too improbable to be anything but a pretence designed to 'suborn' him into behaving in a way that would be at least unhelpful to the revolution. And would Fasnet, after having failed in his design, be likely to give instructions to the 'forces of order' not to seize Henry when he got into the street again after leaving the house? Certainly Fasnet, after crossing the Persian-carpeted hall towards the front door, did not turn aside to go to the telephone, but he perhaps detected apprehension in Henry's face as they stopped at the door, and he said to him,

'I can get in touch with any of my agents at any moment by pocket radio. Just as I could summon one of my household bodyguards electronically in an instant now if you were to distrust and detest me sufficiently to try to rid the earth of me.' Fasnet smiled. 'Well, I must get back to work. I am one of those fortunate persons who don't need or like to sleep for more than three or four hours a night.'

He opened the door for Henry, saying,

'Good luck. And I mean it.'

Outside, the air was cold against Henry's head as he began walking away along the curving gravel drive towards the gate. He realised that he wasn't wearing his corduroy cap. Ingrained unconscious civility (not subservient deference) had caused him to take it off when he had entered Fasnet's mansion. Now he pulled out the cap from his anorak pocket, and as he put it on his head the thought came to him that besides preventing his head from becoming too cold it could also protect him a little if he were to be struck by a policeman's truncheon. Approaching the gate at the end of the gravel drive he became wary. He stopped close up to the gate and leaning over the top of it he glanced quickly up and down the street outside. There were people about, – not so many that he wouldn't have been able to spot a policeman lurking among them, nor so few that there would be no witnesses if one of Fasnet's agents were to attack him. None of the people outside showed interest in him as he opened the gate and came on to the pavement. He stood still, undecided which way he should go. Far down the street to the right he saw high above the roofs of houses the broad white funnel of what could be a very large ship. The docks must be there. He started walking towards them. With shock he soon saw two helmeted policemen quickly approaching him. They drew their batons, but instead of hitting him they turned when they were within a few feet of him and rushed across the road to a stationary car beside the pavement there, and they used their batons to smash its windscreen and then its driver's window, though the driver was still inside the car. Henry did not wait to watch what happened next. He hurried on, almost running, hoping that the policemen would be too preoccupied with their immediate assault to be aware of how he was behaving. After a while he dared to slow down, shakily and breathing hard. Slowly passing an estate agent's show window he noticed two unusual typewriters on display behind it, antique models manufactured no doubt at the beginning of the century. He recognised the window as one he had often seen before and he realised he was in the street where Jack Mabbott lived, an eighty-year-old Communist Party member with whom he had worked during the past few years on various non-Party single-issue campaigns. Jack's house was quite near the estate agent's office, and Henry as he was about to pass Jack's front door had a brief idea of knocking on it, then he remembered how early the morning still was, and he would have walked past the door, but it was suddenly opened by a bare-headed grey-haired man, short and almost militarily upright, who stepped out from it and was Jack Mabbott. Jack gave the impression of having known before opening the door that Henry was passing outside it. Perhaps some precautionary periscopic device was installed inside it enabling him to scan the street first whenever he wanted to leave his house.

'Henry,' he said. 'What are you doing here?'

'I couldn't sleep. I decided I would go for a walk as far as the docks. I wanted to try to make contact with the Resistance.'

Jack, almost as if he hadn't heard Henry mention the Resistance, said only,

'I'm very glad you feel fit enough to get about again. I've been told that you've not been at all well.'

'That's true. But I'm better now. Except for insomnia – and nightmares when I do manage to sleep. What are you up for so early, Jack?'

'I'm going to a meeting. I think you might like to come with me.'

'What meeting?'

'A branch meeting of the Communist Party.'

Henry was silent, and Jack perhaps understood very well that his silence implied a doubt whether the likeliest place for contacting members of the Resistance would be at a meeting of the revisionist British Communist Party. Jack began to move away from the front door near which they had remained standing, and Henry moved with him along the pavement. Jack said,

'I think you might find the Party members at this branch meeting rather different from what you would expect.'

'What do you think I would expect?'

'That they would regard Leninism and violent revolution as having become out of date.'

'Well, yes,' Henry said. 'If they didn't they would be rejecting the political line which the Party has been taking ever since the Second World War.'

'They have rejected it.'

Jack sounded uneasy as he said this. Henry asked quite keenly,

'What line exactly do they want the Party to take?'

'They believe the Party ought to be leading the Resistance – instead of trying to persuade the workers that the occupying power and its British capitalist backers can be defeated by peaceful parliamentary means.'

'Won't the national executive committee expel the branch from the Party?'

'The branch would refuse to accept expulsion, and so would the four other branches in this district. All of them take the same political line as this branch does.'

Henry was beginning to feel a kind of excitement he had felt once or twice before when he had let himself believe that

173

Marxism-Leninism was regaining ground at last in the Party. He knew now that he wanted to go to this meeting. But he said,

'If I do come with you mightn't the branch object to your bringing a non-Party outsider into the meeting?'

'They wouldn't see you as an outsider. They know about you and why you left the Party thirty years ago and they know that your views then were similar to theirs now.'

There seemed an ambivalence in Jack's tone, as if while he was glad at the prospect of being able to bring Henry, a long lapsed member, to a Party meeting again, he was at the same time troubled about the very thing which he knew had made Henry want to come to this meeting – the intention of the branch to defy the Party's national executive committee.

Jack and Henry walked on together without speaking, partly because they saw other people moving in the street now, several of whom were coming towards them along the pavement but passed them without showing any curiosity. Before long Jack turned down into a side street, and Henry followed him. It was a short and narrow street, with a small church, or more probably a Nonconformist chapel, half-way along it and a few yards back from the pavement. Fixed to the stonework just above the chapel porch, was a large oblong yellow board with the words SNOOKER CLUB in red lettering on it. Jack stopped as soon as they had passed the porch, and after looking up and down the side-street towards each of its ends – presumably to make sure there was no one at this moment who was walking across these along either of the two major streets it joined, and who might see him and Henry going into the chapel – he led Henry not to the porch but to a less conspicuous entrance down a tiled path at the side of the chapel.

From the chapel aisle which they came into through this entrance Henry saw that the floor of the nave was occupied

174

by six full-size billiard tables.

'The meeting is in the crypt,' Jack told him. 'The snooker club proprietor is a Party sympathiser who bought the chapel when its congregation became too small to pay for its upkeep as a chapel any longer.'

At the end of the aisle they reached a stone staircase which curved downwards into semi-darkness. Jack said, 'We meet here only in the early mornings – to avoid the risk of being seen by any of the club members.'

As they started descending the stairs a brief remembrance came to Henry of an evening fifty years before when he had gone to make his first contact with the Party. His anxiety then had been about what the Party members would think of him, but now it was more about what he would think of them, and about whether he would be able to feel at one with them as he had felt with his Party comrades in the nineteen thirties.

Just beyond the bottom stair there was a heavy wooden door, which was closed. Jack took hold of the large black iron doorknob and opened the door, and the faces of a group of nine or ten branch members standing under the light of an unshaded electric bulb at the farther end of the crypt turned to look at them. Henry had a momentary impression that two of the faces were of comrades he had known in the Party thirty years before, Enid Palmer and Laurie Gage, but he quickly realised that Enid and Laurie would not be as young now as these two branch members were.

Jack, as he and Henry approached the group, said for them all to hear,

'I've brought comrade Henry Mitchell with me.'

The man who looked like Laurie said to Henry, 'We're glad. Jack has told us about you.' Then he said to Jack, 'Unfortunately the meeting must be postponed. A message has come through from comrade Aminta that Fasnet's

agents are going to explode a large bomb at dawn somewhere near the foreign barracks north of the dockyard. It
isn't intended to do much harm to the barracks, though it
will do a little – and Fasnet won't mind this, as he doesn't
really like the occupying power – but it will destroy quite a
number of working-class homes in the area, and the police
will hope they can credibly accuse the Resistance of being
responsible for it. After the explosion they will be likely to
cordon off the whole district around here and arrest every
leftwinger they can find. We must disperse quite soon.'

An older man who was standing slightly aside from the
rest of the group said,

'There's something I want to say before we go. It won't
take long.' His face, his stance, his voice, seemed extremely
familiar to Henry, and as his age was about the same as
Henry's there was a real possibility that Henry could have
known him in the Party during the nineteen thirties. All at
once Henry remembered with certainty that his name had
been Harry, though nothing else about him, and Harry went
on to say, 'This month fifty years ago I first made contact
with the Party. Two years later I joined it. For sixteen years
after that it was my life. I would not have been able to believe
then that one day while I was still living I would leave it. And
I did not leave it. I did not leave the Party I joined, the Party
of Lenin. I left a party that had betrayed Lenin and would
have expelled me if I hadn't left it. For years since then I
haven't given up hope that the Party of Lenin would rise
again in this country. I am glad to have lived to find this
branch now. I will help you in whatever way I can for as long
as I can.'

He stopped speaking – just in time, Henry thought, to
prevent a break in his voice. He turned and walked away
from the group towards the door of the crypt. Henry had the
feeling of being on the very point of remembering exactly

who he was, but the memory would not come. An urgent wish to talk with a man whose experience of the Party had been so like his own made Henry say to Jack Mabbott, 'I've got to catch him before he gets out of sight.' Jack was surprised, but Henry didn't wait to explain himself to Jack or to the other members of the group. He hurried towards the door of the crypt, hearing as he went the voice of one of them calling out, 'Leave the chapel singly, comrades, and at intervals,' and as he mounted the curving stairs up to the aisle he saw in his mind the disturbed look on Jack's face – the look of someone who had come into the Party years ago because it claimed to stand for principles he believed in, and then had remained faithful to the Party without noticing or wanting to notice it was abandoning those principles and who now when this branch was supporting what the Party had abandoned could not yet be quite sure what he should be faithful to.

At the top of the stairs Henry found that he was short of breath and he warned himself to avoid overstrain, but at the same time he did not want to risk losing track of Harry who was already out of sight and must presumably have left the chapel through the door near the end of the aisle. Luckily, after Henry himself came out to the street along the tiled pathway at the side of the chapel he saw Harry walking away on the pavement not much more than twenty yards ahead of him. Harry was not moving fast and Henry was glad to be able to expect to catch up with him without overexerting himself. The street was long and there was plenty of time. Henry had no thought of danger from the terrorist national police: he was concentrating almost all his attention on Harry in front of him. He noticed after a while that the distance between them had not become any less, so he quickened his pace a little. He began to feel slightly tired. He was glad when he realised that the street they were in was one that led directly back to his own house. He would not have far to walk home after overtaking and talking with Harry. He saw the distant rising slope of the straight street ahead with its lamps on either side converging in upcurved lines towards a high urban horizon and appearing to brighten as the successive intervals from lamp to lamp along the lines became increasingly foreshortened, but there was no longer a gibbous moon between the final houses at the top of the street, and he could not yet see the door of his own house. He seemed to be getting no nearer to Harry in spite of having quickened his pace, so he quickened it still more. After a considerable time he thought he had got a little nearer, though he was very tired now. He took the risk of an immense exertion, which brought him close up behind Harry. Too close. He tripped over one of Harry's feet and he pitched forward on to Harry's back and they both fell heavily down to the pavement. He lost consciousness.

He did not find himself on top of Harry when he became conscious again. He was lying prone on the hard pavement. He raised his head with difficulty and could not see Harry anywhere in front of him. He turned his head with greater difficulty and Harry was not beside him or behind him either. He looked in front of him again and he saw, less than fifty yards ahead past the front doors of several houses, the front door of his own house. He began to crawl painfully forward towards it, flat on the pavement, using his elbows and the inner sides of his knees like an infantryman under fire. But his movement was too slow and the pain too sharp. He would never reach his front door unless he could stand up and walk to it. He tried to lift himself, but he seemed to have a weight, like a bulging outsize military pack, pressing down on his back. It was almost as if he had become Harry and as if his previous self was lying heavily sprawled on top of him. Nevertheless he did at last succeed in getting to his feet. The weight now was no longer on his back but seemed to have become part of his own body. He was able to stumble forward, in a state of semi-consciousness.

He did not know how he reached his front door, or how he found his key to open it, or how he climbed the stairs up to his bedroom, or undressed himself, or finally got back into bed. After he had been lying there for a few minutes he heard a huge explosion somewhere in the town, but he didn't feel capable of leaving his bed again and looking out of his window to discover whether what he had heard had been real or not.